Larceny of the Heart

By

Maxwell Penn

Acknowledgements

To Allah Sakuan who gave me the strength, focus and resolve to complete this daunting task every time I wanted to give up by stating, "You're not gonna write a book !"

To my real just and true brother Darkim Be Allah Christ (www. Famelabsmusic.com)... thanks for saving my life. Guess you knew it was worth saving huh,knowledge seed! Freedom Allah for holding me down in a major way! Eternal Mathematics Allah (Medina Warrior). My P.A.L for eternity Lord Sincere (Pelan). Ishine Allah, Born Everlasting Allah, El Sun Wise Allah,also Universal Allah (Head of Medina). Master K-Bar Allah, Born Perfection Allah, Allah Wise, Supreme Man Allah, and the whole Fame Labs team who supported me and were apart of the sound track for this novel... thanks, let's continue to be pioneers and make history. To my eternal muse Nefertiti...thanks for the insperation. The soundtrack wouldn't have been the same without you, peace queen! To my content editor, Nasira Moore, and her whole staff at Best Part Publishing. Thanks for being super critical and hard on me it made me a better writer. Justice Understanding Allah, Lord Kalim Allah (mean black seed) and the rest of the P.A. crew. King U Self Allah and everybody from down in the D.M.V area who showed me love and respect throughout the years. My home circumference of Queens (represent!!!), and the rest of N.Y.C. . My art director Silver Sterlin (www.Sterlinlife.com and www.myspace.com/crayonmafia) as well as the rest of the Henderson's (E.N.Y) . Ky and all the Headly's (Rochdale), R.I.P. Jax (Neblos). Peace to the Clark family (L.A.) R.I.P. grandma Edna,and Tee. My uncle Gary for making me show and prove my worth as a writer. R.I.P. aunt Elaine (Sadie) the best mother in the world! The Cheathams (Detroit). I also would like to thank all my mentors for your providence and for providing me with the insight and divine light of the supreme teacher and master builder.

Special thanks are also in order to all who support me and purchased my works and every one who I didn't mention who feel as though they should be thanked or acknowledged. I graciously yet humbly thank you all from the very essence and fiber of my being.

Last, however far from least, my enemies (who are great in number). Please keep up the hate! Your weak and wicked mentality continues daily to make me a stronger and better man. Peace, may blessings be upon you all!

Maxwell Penn

CHAPTER ONE

Kingston, Jamaica 1971

One particular morning, Jean Paul Baptiste found himself in a downtown Kingston flea market known as Papine. Being a hustler, it was a place where he should have known he'd end up but he wasn't prepared for the thrill it filled him with. It was money to get here and his palms burned as he looked for a place to set up, still taking in the scene peripherally.

The indoor bazaar was packed. There were booths, tables, elaborate displays, blankets on the floor and even men holding their goods for sale in their hands. The vendors were elbow to elbow but they had everything you could possibly want from clothes to imported luxuries to food, herbs and native medicinal remedies. They even had trinkets and ganja while the customers were eager. The wheeling and dealing was at a fever pitch and the place hummed with business. A few booths over, two men argued congenially over what a radio was worth. They had a circle of people around them and whenever one scored a point in his argument, his supporters let out a loud cheer. When, at last, the haggler was given a price he could live with, he waved the radio triumphantly in the air and others surged forward with their own money for the same deal.

The money flowed. British pounds, as well as Jamaican and American currency. The papers and coins made their own music and Jean was ready for the dance.

"How much for the painting in the front?"

He still had his back turned, was just done setting up when the question was posed. The man was an American, by his accent. He looked over Jean's work appreciatively and the beautiful lady on his arm smiled from ear to ear, obviously the person who'd called his attention to the large canvasses and sculptures of every size Jean had laid out. She wasn't the one with the money. Jean could read people well enough to know that but he could also look at the short Black man in front of him and see she didn't need her own money...she had his. The pudgy tourist's arm tightened around her waist and she pointed at another hand painted portrait of a sunset at Jean's feet. He went to work.

"I wasn't going to sell this one," Jean Paul lied, taking down the picture the tourist had pointed to. He stood it against the side of another as though he were trying to hide it. "But this one," he picked up the painting of the sunset the lady was staring at and held it up in front of her. "This one, I will sell for two thousand dollars."

"Two thousand dollars?" The man screamed. He let go of the woman and stepped forward, adjusting his glasses. "That's utterly ridiculous!"

Jean laughed. "No sir, you don't understand. That's only fifty of your American dollars. Here in yard, one American dollar is worth roughly forty dollars."

The woman's face brightened and she slapped the tourist playfully on his arm. "I can't take him anywhere," she said, stroking his ego as if he were a tough guy. He laughed sheepishly and his arm went back around her slim waist.

"Thank you so much, my friend," he said to Jean. "You just saved me a whole mess of trouble. We just got here and imagine how many fights I would have gotten into not knowing the rate of exchange."

Perhaps Jean was underestimating the pudgy tourist but he couldn't picture him in a fight at all. He smiled at the lady now. "If it's a hardship to you, my American friend, I can go lower."

The tourist took the bait. "It's no hardship at all," he said. "It's quite a beautiful piece but friend, what about the other one? The first one my wife picked out?"

Jean made a series of faces. He handed the painting of the sunset to the tourist then picked up the one he'd reluctantly put off to the side. He scrutinized the painting then, biting the side of his mouth, began his spiel. "I made this painting a year ago, during carnival. I sold the other painting, in the same tones, to another American... a very important man, for one hundred American dollars." He made a face like this was an unbelievable sum of money, as though he expected the tourist and his lady to also be impressed. "At the time, he wanted this one also but I wasn't able to complete it in time. I wanted it to be perfect," he looked proudly at the picture. "And now, I am waiting for him to return to the island, as he does every year. He is a very, very, very important man... maybe someone in your government, maybe a rich businessman or one of your best doctors. A very rich and important man. He will buy this painting for one hundred American dollars as well. It is not a hardship to him."

The tourist's face clouded and Jean knew he had played his cards right. After that, the man's ego wouldn't allow him to not buy it, whatever the cost. "What if he doesn't come, my friend? Business is business. You can't turn away a paying customer now for one who might not come later."

He took a thick black billfold from the rear pockets of his shorts.

"Do you want it, darling?" He asked the lady.

"Absolutely, honey. It is so beautiful. Both of them are." She looked at Jean. "You are so talented. You would be one of the world's most famous with the right training. Where did you study?"

Jean wanted to close the deal, not go off on a tangent. "At my father's knee," he said jokingly. She laughed but he returned his attention to the black billfold. "Sir, I have others. I have that one. I can sell you this," he picked up an oil painting he'd done of the docks at the pier. It was a totally different scheme from what the lady had picked and he knew it wouldn't suffice. "This one, for half of that. I..."

The tourist shook his head feverishly, deaf to whatever else Jean had to say. He had to have the $100 painting whose twin had been bought by the rich and important American. In his mind, Jean was a rube who had been wowed by a honeymooner with a couple hundred dollars. But, Jean had no idea how wealthy and important he was. He'd show him real class. In the tourist's mind, he suspected Jean could not fathom him having money because he was a black man and that desperately made the tourist want to prove him wrong.

"My friend, we'll take both of these. Wrap them for me and we will pick them up on our way back to our hotel. This," he removed four fifty dollar bills from his wallet and placed them in Jean's hand. "This is for the paintings and a little tip for you, to get some new oils and brushes and things of that nature." He said with a slight grin.

Jean didn't have to pretend. He was genuinely speechless. "Oh. Oh, my. Two hundred dollars? I…"

The tourist had "won". He was thoroughly enjoying Jean's stupor and awe at the amount he'd so casually given. With his chest puffed out he clapped Jean on the shoulder. "We'll be back later my friend."

The lady gave him a little wave then arm in arm, they walked off , leaving an ecstatic young man in their wake.

On the beach, Jean had sold his work for 20 or 30 American dollars, at most. For a beautiful lady or someone who really and truly loved a particular piece, he'd go even lower and sometimes accepted barter.

He'd done well for himself though, even with the discounts he gave to honeymooners and natives. He had no kids, no wife and was making out like a bandit. But $200.00? In his first fifteen minutes of work? He would have never imagined it.

His most trusted friend on the island, Paul Chin, who everyone called Chinaman, had given him the heads up after visiting Papine. "You would kill them in there, bredren." He'd said, laughing at Jean's ability to sell anything, one day on the beach.

Jean trusted Chinaman but he'd been nervous about changing his spot, content with what he was getting on the beach. It was a gamble, as most would assume the tourists would flock to the resorts on the island's North coast, to the white sand beaches with their crystal clear blue waters, or to Ocho Rios, Negril and Montego Bay while never venturing into the island's interior. But Jamaica's sultry beauty, its rich countryside, rolling mountains, infinite coconut and palm trees and many winding rivers had their own magnetism and they were drawn. The hospitality of the natives and the allure of authentic artisan crafts enticed them further. Tourists roamed every mile of the island. Papine had been a gamble but he could feel, instinctively, that something had led him there especially if there was money to be made.

Jean left the market on cloud nine. His pockets bulged and the cart he'd bought his paintings and sculptures on was much lighter than when he'd come in. Outside, he and the small group of friends he'd made throughout the day blended in with the throngs of islanders making their way home through Kingston's streets. They chatted amicably about the day. Jean had a naturally likable air about him and he never had a problem meeting new comrades. He was a hustler, yes, but honorable and principled in his conduct and men found him trustworthy and reasonable. His sharpness and wit also ranked him a natural comedian. The ladies were not so concerned with any of that . Too often they were dazed by the way he looked like a God of love sculpted in chocolate. His dark brown eyes and their thick lashes were what women called "bedroom eyes" and he had learned early that he could seduce women from afar just by fixing his gaze on them. They would come to him, run their hands over his hard muscular arms and chest, whisper softly while touching his long, taut hands, that they'd always had a thing for artists. And he would reciprocate, confessing to them that artists also had a thing for them...

It was this attraction for him that landed the twenty one year old in Jamaica about two and a half years earlier. Jean had turned into something of a playboy back in Haiti. After one too many mothers with their ruined daughter in tow came knocking on his door, he'd been shipped to the hinterland - the interior of Haiti, where his parents had friends. Jean was miserable there. Between the boredom and never ending chores he lost his mind after three days and ran away. When he arrived back home two days later, parched famished and exhausted, his mother sucked her teeth at the sight of him and slammed the door in his face. His parents both thought he was headed down the wrong road. In a country with very serious consequences for all of life's mistakes, they were not overreacting.

Jean barely had time to think through his plight when a fat old truck zoomed past, coughing and squealing. It died a smokey death on the horizon. By the time Jean reached the cab, its human contents, a Soca band from St. Lucia, stood on the side of the road. Jean had been working on trucks like that with his father from infancy. Within the hour, he had the truck back on the road. As a token of their gratitude, the band offered him a job as a handy man and passage with them to any destination of his choosing. He'd toured the entire Caribbean, tomcatting and sampling the delights of every shore, sowing his young oats and breaking hearts of many young beautiful women along the way. However, when his feet touched the soil of Jamaica, the lovely island of water and wood, his heart was captured and he knew he was there for a purpose. He had family on the island his grandparents, he'd been told, lived in the parish of Trelawney. He'd gone to look for them in his mother's home town of Wakefield, but once he reached the address he had for them that he'd memorized since a child, the residents there told him that he must have been talking about the couple who died in a hurricane ten years before they bought the house.

Jean was saddened to find out of his grand parents demise, however he'd earned a decent amount of money touring with the Soca band he'd come to Jamaica with or at least enough to start getting himself established in his new environment.

By and by, his companions made their way home and he did as well. He managed to make it to the city and lease a small flat in Kingston's Salt Lane section. It was a clean but efficient studio with room for his paints and canvasses and a comfortable bed. It lacked flourish but it was more than enough for the young bachelor and his female guests. Jean ate a plate of food he'd bought at the Papine market and then showered and dressed in his Friday night best, in preparation for a session at a local dancehall that night.

When Jean arrived at the party, he was greeted by his crew of casual acquaintances. Other young men he played dominoes with or knew from here or there and his best and one true friend in Jamaica. Paul Chin who was better known in the streets of Kingston as Chinaman. He'd met China the first day he'd stepped foot in Kingston and they instantly hit it off. China was like a brother to him and the feeling was mutual. Jean was a very magnetic individual and people seemed to always gravitate to him so he had many acquaintances but no one he trusted and respected as much as China. China was a man of his word, a soldier.

He didn't have a false bone in his body and time and time again had proven himself to be the type of comrad a man could rely on.

At five foot eleven, China stood a couple of inches shorter than Jean. He had dark brown skin, curly locks of black hair, chubby cheeks and slightly slanted eyes due to his mixed Chinese and black heritage.

"What a gwaan my youth?" Jean greeted him. His friend smiled, clasped his hand.

"Nuthin a gwaan, jus a cool now breda." They watched the crowd moving through the dancehall. "Come now Jean, the two a we a go bun a spliff of sinsi, seen?" China spoke over the music.

They walked to a dark corner of the dancehall by one of the loudspeakers that were vibrating the bass of the latest Bob Marley and the Wailers tune. Twenty minutes later, nothing was left of the spliff but ashes and a good vibe between friends.

The party was in a dancehall; nothing too fancy, just a moderate sized one story brick building with a wooden floor, a bar in the middle of the room and space for about four hundred people. They had it filled by twice its capacity. The selector threw on the latest studio one record and the crowd rushed the floor. Jean and China stood there, drinking Stouts and vibing to the beat, posing for the lovelies when the urge struck them.

Although in each one's mind, he was by far the better looking of the two. They both enjoyed the affections of the opposite sex and often engaged in a friendly competition to see who could get the most girls anywhere they were. That night would be no different. They stood there absorbing the atmosphere of the party until the high went down a little and they each spotted a lovely they wanted to make a move on.

One found China first and as she let him know she liked what she was seeing with a serious come-hither glance. Jean nudged him towards her with his elbow and went to go take a leak. He made his way through the standing room only crowd and, after about 10 minutes, he finally made it to the restroom. He was about three feet away when he accidentally rubbed up against a young lady who was standing alongside the wall by herself with her arms folded across her chest in a defensive looking position.

The girl was beautiful! She stood about five foot seven, had small curly locks of silky auburn and black hair with golden copper toned skin. Her almond shaped eyes and supple, pouty round lips competed with her powerful yet infinite legs that just wouldn't quit Her robust and firm chest as well as her backside made Jean's mouth water. Her tresses were highlighted with a single red rose pinned to the left side of her head and a decoration. In addition, her perfect coke bottle shape lured him with an attraction he'd never felt before. Even though he'd conquered some of the most dazzling women of the

Caribbean, this particular specimen was by far the most exotic beauty he'd ever laid his eyes on. He likened her to Nefertiti, Sheeba or another majestic Ethiopian empress. He couldn't believe how beautiful she was and that such a beautiful angel could be here on Earth. Instantly, he felt that fate caused them to meet, even if only by causing him to bump against her for a brief moment.

Jean placed his hand on her bare shoulder, not too far from the strap that was holding up her form hugging, one piece red dress. It was a gesture to convey how sorry he felt for bumping into her. "So sorry baby love… mi never mean to bump you still," Jean spoke into her ear, striving to be heard over the music.

The beautiful young woman smiled at him courteously and shook her head up and down, acknowledging that everything was quite alright.

When Jean had leaned over to whisper in her ear, he'd smelled her sweet perfume and it only heightened the trance like state he felt himself falling into. He was intoxicated by her beauty and her whole package. Jean found himself caught up so he just stood there for a second staring at her before he snapped himself out of it and came back with a few questions in his best Don Juan voice once again.

"Can I have a dance with you?" Jean asked as his brain was almost frozen by the ravishing beauty's captivating looks.

"I'm sorry but I'm waiting for my boyfriend. He went to the bathroom and will be out any second now." The beautiful stranger replied, leaning forward to where Jean could hear her.

"That's a shame that we can't dance tonight...but true I tell you this...your boyfriend is one lucky man!" Jean said into her ear.

"Thank you." She replied with a smile and a look of being flattered on her perfect face.

"Well listen, if I mon cannot have a dance with you this evening, can I at least know the name of the most gorgeous looking woman on the whole island of Jamaica?"

With a wider smile and a little giggle, the woman said "Winsome." into Jean's eager left ear.

Before Jean could say another word, a tall caramel complected man came up behind her and grabbed the young girl by her hand. Shooting Jean a dirty look before making his way with her back to the crowded dance floor. Jean felt the flash of bad vibes from him and his reaction was more dramatic than it had to be. He'd snatched the girl away as though he might hit her or Jean, rather than the way a man who knows he has a good looking woman casually steps back into the frame when he sees another like minded soul making his advances.

Jean stood there for another moment, still dazed by the woman and the desire she'd sparked in him. Despite the heat and sundry scent of liquor, jerk chicken and ganja in the air, all Jean could smell was the enticing scent of her perfume. He was completely smitten with her. Eventhough, she'd just left holding hands with another man. Jean made up his mind that his singular mission had just become to take her away from the man she was with and to make her his. Maybe it was the way her boyfriend reacted, or maybe it was the way he smelled or the way he looked. Whatever it was, Jean determined that the slim young beauty would be his…

He'd never had a problem winning the heart of any young woman he'd set his sights on and therefore never had been in this quandary. He'd never been out to take another man's girl before but something about her was so different, so beautiful and seductive, that he made no effort to restrain his lust. Maybe, he was turned on by the challenge of her belonging to another. Maybe, he simply wanted to test his powers of seduction. Or maybe, it was some instinctive knowledge that she too felt the same attraction he did. He taxed his brain trying to figure it all out but gave up content to remember the way she fit into her tight red dress instead. Whatever it was, he acknowledged it as he remembered why he was there and opened the door to the restroom. However, he would stop at nothing to have the beautiful Winsome in his arms.

The party progressed as most others did and, after a time, Jean, China and some other friends went outside to smoke more herb. They were discussing the women in the dancehall and who each one was eyeing but Jean did not mention the fierce brown beauty who'd captured his heart. Even when she emerged from the party still in the grip of the tall man who grabbed her earlier, he didn't say a word. He motioned towards them with a nod until China gave him a nod back confirming he'd noted the couple. They came through the crowd like celebrities and Jean had his first glimpse of how hard his chosen task would be. Her man was evidently "somebody" judging by the way people made sure to speak to him and waited anxiously for him to acknowledge them in return. When he reached where they stood, the caramel complected man smiled and touched fists with Chinaman in greeting and then walked to a car that came for them from around the corner. Without any concern for the beautiful young woman who trailed in tow, he opened his own door and got in, leaving her to let herself in on the other side.

Jean shook his head and laughed in disgust at his brashness and arrogance, knowing he would soon make the careless boyfriend pay dearly for it.

"My youth, you know the bwoy with the gal deh, who just got into the car?" Jean asked.

"Yeah mon, that's Dexter. I work with his father at the bauxite mine. Him father is the foreman there."

Jean noted the caution in his friend's voice but grinning devilishly, decided to ignore it. "Who is that gal? Is that really his girl with him deh?"

"Dexter have alot of gals you know, but he been movin with her for at least a year now...but me never know if she is his main girl still."

"Me nah care," Jean announced. "Dat no matter mi if she his main girl or not. That gal I must have, she gon be mine one day soon. Watch!"

Chinaman shook his head. He laughed at his moon struck friend, willing him to avoid the drama which would no doubt ensue.

The car took off and the show was over. The two friends bid farewell to the group, weaving their way through the crowd in search of the set of young women that would come home with them that evening.

Not much later, they each had a beautiful and willing young thing. As he made his way, the girl on Jean's arm home was a ten and perfect in every way but, in his mind, she was a meager substitute for the lovely and mysterious Winsome.

The next morning, after the girls had left, Jean probed China for information about beauty from the club, begging his friend to tell him everything he knew about her.

"Well, like I say, Dexter has many girls...she just happen to just be one. He treat her like his one and only so anything Dexter says to do, she jumps for him. I had a crush on her older sister Gwen when we were younger and I went to school with Winsome as a pickny and I hear that Gwen moved to foreign a few years back and that Winsome still live with her mama. If they still live in the same house from when we was growing up. Then she lives up town on Red Hills Road, in Kingston Six." He explained but that was all he had so they changed the topic. They shot the breeze a little while longer then China went home and Jean went into town to go pay his respects to the local constable.

Jean wasn't legal on the island and couldn't get a license to vend. He was tired of being harassed and threatened with jail or having his goods and money taken. Constable Brown, a.k.a Bigga, was a fat giant of a man who stood six foot five inches tall and three hundred sixty pounds. His jet black skin was punctuated with blackheads scars and boils. This was all capped off by a face only a mother could love and loose floppy ears. Bigga wanted twelve hundred dollars every two weeks or roughly $60.00 American dollars a month. For that, Jean could live in peace and sell where ever he pleased. Jean thought it was a small price to pay.

"Morning John!" The big man greeted in his deep gruff mono toned voice as Jean came into the restaurant where they always met. The constable pronounced Jean's name this way deliberately as not to let on his true nationality. During his stay in Jamaica, Jean found that people genuinely liked him until they found out he was of Haitian decent. He never understood some native Jamaicans deep rooted hatred for Haitians. He figured that in essence they were all the same. He decided to use the English name of "John" while on the island as not to make waves, and so he could just fit in. Bigga had a feast before him of porridge, porgie fish, callalou, and a dumpling. Jean slid into the booth with him, nodding in acknowledgement of the other men in the place. Many nodded back or simply touched their hats. Satisfied that he'd been mannerly, he turned back to Bigga.

"Morning, Bigga."

He took an envelope out of his pocket and slid it to him. "Count it." This was somewhat of a game between the two of them. Jean never had any qualms about trying to haggle with Bigga over the amount of his extortion. But, on that day, he had all the money in the envelope and then some. "I don't have to see you for a month now!" He laughed, triumphantly.

Bigga opened it good naturedly, pleased when he saw what the envelope held. He liked "John." It was hard not to like him. The young man was smart, funny and had an easy way. But, this is how business was done. One hand washed the other. I do something for you, you do something for me and in the fickle Caribbean economy. It was all about making or taking a buck.

"This is good John," Bigga said, smiling.

Jean looked into his beady eyes and knew there was bad news to follow. "But?"

He looked away then picked his teeth with his fingers as he burped and patted his big belly. "Please excuse," he said, making a sucking sound with the food in his mouth. Jean rolled his eyes at Bigga's show of politeness. The big man laughed. They both knew Bigga had no manners. "See what happen...Like I said before... I like you... but I'm getting a lot of heat from my boys down at immigration. They is rassing with me bout bringing in more illegal aliens and its getting harder and harder, everyday, to keep them away from you and sending you back where you come from."

"Bigga," Jean started. He knew this was all bullshit. "I'm Jamaican too you know."

Bigga nodded sympathetically and belched loudly again. "Yes, mi know you is a yard mon at heart and it's nothing personal; but, you must help me make it easier from them harassing me..."

"A lie you tell"

"John, I know, I know, but they coming down hard on me now. John, I'm the constable but even I have people that I must answer to. So…"

"A lie, you tell Bigga."

He could see he was wearing Bigga down and that the fat man's conscience was bothering him about what he was trying to do.

"So John, I figure to still keep you safe, it would be worth at least another, ahh, four hundred dollars, a month-"

"Fuckry, pure fuckry, fuckery a gwaan."

"John, what can I mon do, its the immigration-"

"Pure fucrky Bigga."

"Three hundred then, John, it's the lowest I can go, I have the pressures. "Bigga, why? Why you do this kind of thing. What's wrong with you, Bigga…"

Jean was a natural born salesman and he was about to sell water to a well. He was going to make Bigga back down and lower his bribe rates. He watched the fat man's face to see what angle he could take. "Bigga…"

Suddenly, the door of the restaurant opened with a boom. Everyone in the small, homey feeling eatery stopped and turned to look. It was a tall, expensively dressed man with a woman at his side. He stood between Jean and the girl so that Jean didn't see the girl the caramel complected man directed rudely to a table. The fellow picked over the crowd visually, selecting those he felt were worthy of acknowledgement and shouting to them or giving them hearty handshakes. He walked through the restaurant as though he owned it and there was almost a dare in his arrogant swagger.

Everyone looked different, all of a sudden shook up. He also saw clearly that some of the faces bore the faintest trace of disgust but no one dared meet the boy's gaze.

"What a gwaan, Dex?" Bigga's voice no longer bore any trace of playfulness and his expression had hardened as well. The boy was doing his best to ignore Jean who now sipped his tea as he waited for him to finish speaking to Bigga and be on his way. The young man countered this snub by situating himself into the booth as well. When he sat, Jean looked him right in the eye and the boy flinched first, looking away as though he were intently focused on Bigga.

"Cool runnings, mon... every ting crisp, sorry I'm a little late." He went into his pocket and with no attempt to be discreet handed Bigga a roll of money. Bigga looked at the money with disbelief then after doing a quick visual survey of the room, put the knot in his pocket.

"Dexter, this is my bwoy, John... John, this here is Dexter Vassel, the don of Kingston Six!" The chief said this in a deep booming voice as he patted the pocket with the tall guy's money. It was theatrical and Jean noted the insincerity in Bigga's speech.

"How you mean the don?" Jean quizzed with a false sense of naïveté. He'd placed the joker. It was the same guy from the dancehall uptown.

"What he mean is that I run a large part of all the local bad mon business and ganja trade in the area and since you're here. He's either got some dirt on you as well or you is a constable undercover yourself!"

Dexter stated loud enough for every one in the restaurant to hear him and stood then, as though daring Jean. All eyes in the restaurant were on them and Jean saw that everyone looked uncomfortable and that Bigga's face had turned to stone.

He decided to shut "Dex" down.

Jean smiled. "Or my youth, it could mean that I'm just here in a restaurant, speaking to an esteemed constable of Kingston! In the company of good men and elders." He nodded to the elderly men who sat in the corner at the first tables of the restaurant having breakfast and drinking their coffee. He couldn't believe that Dexter had spoken so loosely, in such a public place. The men here all had something to lose. No one could quite withstand being accused publicly of being in a den of bad mon and ganja peddlers.

Silently, the men's eyes trained on Jean and he saw small but passionate nods of approval and outright shouts of assent, then men standing in solidarity, openly supporting Jean in the confrontation. He continued, "Patriots... and men of reason, scholars. In such highly regarded company, my youth, it could simply mean I'm having a cup of tea with a friend." At this, he slurped his tea loud, with one pinkie in the air, and everybody in the restaurant burst out laughing.

Bigga clapped him hard across the back, shaking his whole frame. Shooting him a dirty look of disapproval, Dexter nodded to Jean like he would hurt him but he wasn't worth the bother. Then, he shook hands with Bigga and walked to the bar and collected his lady friend. Jean didn't give them a second look. He got back to the business of trading barbs and negotiating a better agreement with Bigga.

He had already decided what to do about the woman he'd seen Dexter with last time. She was going to be his. He just knew, when everyone else laughed at Dexter, and ridiculed her man, she would throw her head back and laugh. He felt, almost imagined that in his peripheral sight. In his mind's eye, the lilting sound of her laughter carried louder and higher than the gruff snickers of the old men around her.

CHAPTER TWO

"You see him, John? He's a smart youth too. He knows how to run business and treat his people right, seen? Me and my cousin used to run with his father when we were younger before his old man became big time. Then, he took over the bauxite mine. We done business for years. I go way back with his family." Bigga said, somberly as though he were trying to explain something rather than reminiscing about old friends.

However, Jean couldn't care less. He'd been thinking about his grandparents and his coming back to Jamaica to find his roots. He wouldn't let himself be dissuaded.

Bigga watched the door Dexter had just gone through with a look of worry under the surface. Jean stood up then hoisted his large green duffel bag over his shoulder. He shook hands with Bigga and turned his back to start making his way to the door. Bigga signaled to the waitress and as she came over to take his next order, he said while laughing to Jean, "That's right my bwoy, gwaan out there so and make our money."

Jean gave him a dirty look and the middle finger. "Fuck you Bigga, fuck you." He said, laughing.

Jean made his way to Papine and set up for the day. With another party Saturday evening fresh on his mind, the next several days went by swiftly. In that short three day span, he had managed to profit the equivalent of one hundred American dollars. He made out like a bandit that weekend. One hundred American dollars was a bundle of cash at that time in the Caribbean while Jean was making a phenomenal, unbelievable sum of money and, had he been a more materialistic sort of person, he would have been very flashy and overbearing with his earnings. Instead, he had the mentality of a young bachelor trying to enjoy life and have a good time. Besides, being new to Kingston and extra flashy would only make him a target to those suffering in the ghetto. And, in those times, there was no shortage of bandits willing to take what you had if you were doing too much flashing and weren't strong enough to safeguard your goods. He saved the vast majority of his earnings and managed to amass about eight thousand American dollars in the two and a half years he'd been in Jamaica.

Jean took the money he'd made over the last several days and purchased himself an outfit for the session. He bought himself an Italian silk button down shirt, a fresh pair of crisp linen slacks and the latest top notch British shoes. Then, he went to the barber and got a proper haircut.

When China met up with him at his flat that evening, after giving a girl named Suzette back shots all afternoon and then changing into his finest wears for the party, he took one look at Jean and whistled. "Bwoy, you a go kill them tonight with your style and fashion."

Jean knew he looked sharper than a stiletto blade. He sprayed himself with the finest cologne and answered with playful modesty, "Well, I try to do what I can, you know..."

They shared a laugh and soon left, making their way to where the session was being held in Kingston Two.

Because the vast majority of people in Jamaica didn't have television or telephone at that time, the dancehall session was a very important place. It was the place to be seen, to come in tune with friends and peers and to catch up on the news and all the goings-ons. Jean desperately wanted to be a somebody in Kingston even if it was for one night out of the week when he attended a session. Depending what sound set was playing, rival factions would occasionally clash and end up having shootouts, causing sheer pandemonium to break out when the whole dance hall would stampede.

Jean and Chinaman had good instincts and had never even been close to getting trampled or catching a stray shot. And despite whatever dangers, after working like a slave in the street all week, to look and live like a king, even if it were only for that moment, made the rest of the week worth living. Many young Jamaicans wouldn't miss the action of the dancehall for anything in the world.

This particular venue was on Windward Road, in a dancehall that had a tiled floor, a vast open floor plan, a bar in the middle of the dance floor and a patio in the back. Huge fans whirred overhead, hanging by steel poles from the tin ceiling but it was still sizzling hot in the place. The dancehall was made for five hundred people but held the heat of at least a thousand bodies.

The crowd was in a fever pitch as the selector threw on the latest dub plate and began to chat rhythmically to the record. His accent was deep but the rhythm was so precise that the crowd was electric. Jean could feel it in the air that this was going to be a night to remember.

As he scoped the crowd pressed together on the patio, his eyes came to rest on one person in particular. He rolled his eyes when he saw clearly who it was. Dexter. He looked away in annoyance, wondering why he was seeing this clown everywhere now. After their last meeting at the restaurant, he'd had time to think about it and realized that he hated the man's style. In Jean's eyes, for all of his jewelry, swagger and arrogance, Dexter wasn't anybody. Sure he had nice clothes, but in Jean's eyes, he wasn't wearing them right. He'd gotten into a beautiful car, but he didn't look good doing it. Even the girl on his arm didn't look right on his particular arm…the man had money but style didn't suit him.

Jean danced to a few sets then the music began to fade and the crowd on the patio began to thin out a little to the backyard as a lover's rock tune boomed through the enormous homemade speakers. Everyone who could grab someone to dance with made their way to the patio or backyard, coupled up. As China pulled a girl named Clintonia to the dance floor in a slow drag, Jean, who hadn't been quick enough to grab the girl he'd been eyeing, made his way to the bar for a few Red Stripes.

He played the bar, scoping the crowd for his next victim. Just as it was getting good, after his eyes had fallen on one delectable, enticing and sensual beauty after another and he was feeling like this was the best party in a long time. His eyes fell on Dexter again. This time, he was dancing with a girl. Jean felt himself filling with disgust the more he stared at him, but he just couldn't look away.

With his hand possessively at her waist, Dexter and the girl grinded methodically to the mellow baseline. Then, his hands began to travel, slowly up her back to her shoulder blades, molding and caressing the silken brown skin. He played with the straps of her dress at her neck intimately as if he were preparing to disrobe her. The two of them moved slowly, passionately to the beat and Dexter's hands began to stroke her again. When they reached the woman's firm round bottom, he opened his hands and palmed them urgently, pressing her to him as though he owned it.

As Dexter and the girl turned to the rhythm, they switched sides and Jean had a bird's eye view of who was dancing with Dexter. It was the beautiful Winsome. Dexter continued to caress her and mold her body to his. She looked like a toy in his arms, his toy.

Jean felt a flood of emotions. He felt angry and part of him wanted to rush the floor and break the two of them apart. His jealousy made him want to grab Winsome and show Dexter up, put on a demonstration of his own to rival; whatever, the joker thought he had done. He wanted to break both of the Dexter's arms off and beat him down with them. He wanted to fall down from the ceiling on the two of them and wrestle his adversary to the ground, then dance on his chest with the lovely Winsome. His jealousy riled him until he felt dizzy, and nauseated.

The two of them left the dance floor and jostled through the crowd, making their way towards him. He got to study Winsome as she approached and marveled at the way her body graced the beautiful halter dress she wore. Her hourglass shaped body filled it out to perfection and the stiletto heels she wore accentuated the longness of her tawny legs. The open toed shoes added to her height and she looked regal, as though she were floating above everyone else there. Her crown of hair was decorated with another red rose and she wore a gold choker at her neck. Their eyes met as he watched her and he saw a flicker there before she looked away.

Jean smiled to himself, thinking although Dexter had control of her body on the dance floor, he held her in his heart. China reached him with Clintonia and her friend Carla in tow. The smile on his face let him know that China had verified they were down to go back to Jean's house and be entertained after they left the dancehall. They sat at the bar for a moment, drinking beers and smooth talking the girls. The vibe of the night had been righteous. The girls were beautiful and good company and Jean was floating on cloud nine, feeling eerie.

The music boomed around them and the crowd was live. There was an excitement in the air and Jean had the sense once again that something was about to happen. He scoped the scenery around him, taking stock of where he was. Everyone looked vibrant in their finery and the air was filled with a million perfumes and the laughter of a thousand jokes and tales. Carla was telling him an entertaining story about her father. Clintonia leaned into China as she talked to him, her hands casually resting on his leg. China looked over at Jean and gave him a nod towards the patio.

Without asking, Jean knew he wanted to burn something and he eased Carla along behind his friend and her girl. They were at a table, smoking the spliff when the chaos broke out. Jean heard voices raised and the crowd surged. He stood up to see what was happening and, at that moment, caught sight of Dexter and Winsome again. The sensual passion on display the last time he'd seen them was gone, replaced by searing anger.

Dexter stood over her threateningly. He was yelling in her face and flaying his arms as though he was going to hit her. Jean knew something crazy was about to happen now that he'd spotted them having an argument in public. He slowly made his way to the bar in their direction with Chinaman following his lead.

Without thinking, Jean found himself walking towards them, determined to prevent what was about to happen. China reached out to stop him. It wasn't worth it. The girl wasn't his relation or acquaintance and therefore not his concern but it was too late. His friend pushed though the crowd like a man possessed and Chinaman had no choice but to follow behind him and try and keep him from getting himself killed. These were dangerous people and he didn't know what the hell Jean was thinking.

They were less than five feet away when, with a flick of his arm, Dexter sent a drink flying up into Winsome's face. She gasped and shrank away, wiping her face and Dexter made a move towards her with his right hand opened and arm cocked back...then he slapped her. "Bitch ah mi Dexter you can't tell I what fi do. I'm a don Bitch! You hear that bitch a don... you dog! You're nothing, me a don!"

The man whose drink Dexter had thrown stood there, livid. Before he could say a word, a wild looking dread from Dexter's posse pulled out a black Magnum. The gun's barrel flashed onyx as he raised it. Then, the silver of white heat laced the guns mouth as he began firing.

The crowd surged again in a panic and Jean fought harder to get to Winsome. The force of the inflicted blow caused Winsome's head to turn totally in the other direction. It stung so bad she swore her face was engulefed in fire!

Dexter was distracted by the new development and his attention turned now to insulting and threatening the man whose drink he'd thrown.

Jean placed a soft hand on Winsome's shoulder and guided her away from the fray. "Let me get you to a taxi. Get you home!" He shouted over the music. The gunfire had caused a near stampede but some brave hearts still lingered. The women in the dancehall had retreated to its depths, trying to get a good view of the melee without being in the crossfire.

Winsome was aware of all of them as she wiped her face and tried to focus her eyes. She knew it was the handsome stranger from the party a few weeks earlier who was speaking to her but even this didn't give her comfort. She felt the rage broiling inside her and hatred for Dexter Vassel flashed in her soul. He had treated her like a common whore for the last time. She was tired of his abuse and his flagrant disrespect. He had no character and all of his power was based on the fear men had of his father, Donavan Vassel, a real gangster. Dexter was merely a brat playing at being a don. She had stomached his rudeness for far too long and, when she saw the way the other women were whispering and snickering, her realization of that turned into a burning desire for revenge. She wanted to disrespect and humiliate him as much as he had done to her time and time again.

She wiped her face clear and then turned to the stranger. "Yes, please. Thank you." She let him take her arm and walked close to him, past the gawkers. Some of these women had wanted Dexter for years, others had pretended to be her friend to get close and find out her business. If Jean hadn't come to her rescue, they would have watched and laughed while Dexter beat her bloody in the dancehall. She held her head up high as she exited the dancehall, aware that many pairs of eyes followed their departure.

CHAPTER THREE

Ten minutes later, they were in a cab headed up to Red Hills Road where Winsome lived. Even though things were in a foul state of affairs that evening, Jean loved the peaceful look on Winsome's face as she took a cat nap in the cab on the way home. About twenty minutes later, the cab arrived in front of the address she had given the driver. Jean gently nudged Winsome on the shoulder, with his right hand seemingly sinking into her butter soft skin. She came to, thanked Jean for his help and then bid him good evening as she walked through the gates of her yard. Jean told the taxi driver to wait a few moments to make sure she got into her house safely. It wasn't until they'd pulled off again, this time on the way to his flat in Salt Lane that he noticed Winsome had accidentally left her pocket book in the car.

At about three the next afternoon, Chinaman was knocking at Jean's door. They greeted each other and then Jean invited China indoors. China revealed that as far as he knew no one had been hurt last night. The only thing that got hurt was his sex life because he'd missed the chance to link up with Clintonia that evening. China wanted to know if they were going to play dominoes like they did every Sunday.

"Yeah mon, right after I go and give Miss Winsome her pocketbook, because she left it inna cab from last night," Jean replied.

"Yeah mon...me never seen Dexter act like that because of no girl...or at least not in front of so many people like that. He told me Winsome caught him fucking a next gal, and she kept asking him about that inna party last night... the next thing you know, it caan done!!! Seen? My bwoy, after that, you just might even have a chance with she." China stated only half joking.

Jean told China that he would meet him back at his flat at five that evening. Right then and there, his main focus was getting Winsome back her purse, scoring some more brownie points and getting on her good side.

An hour and a half later, Jean rolled on to Red Hills Road on his two wheeled motorbike. Jean never had a reason to visit the neighborhood before and he was impressed with the size and beauty of the homes he saw. They were palaces compared to the ghetto areas of Kingston.

He found the house and made his was anxiously to her front door. He was so nervous that the closer he got, the further away the door seemed. Finally, he knocked on the door and a second later, Winsome flung in open, clad in only her nightgown and a partially open robe.

"So mama, you forgot your..." Winsome began before realizing it was Jean Paul and not whoever she'd been speaking to at the door. She'd thought it was her mother. After all, no one came to visit on Sundays because she was in church most of the day. Dexter might have come by but she just knew after the night before that she and Dexter over with so it couldn't be him.

When she saw the mysterious and handsome stranger from the dance hall at her doorstep, she very quickly closed her robe and hid behind the door, quizzing coyly. "Yes, sir may I help you?"

Jean replied in a school-boyish fashion that was almost totally out of character. "Yes, well mi lady. It seems as if you left your pocketbook in the back seat of the cab last night!"

Winsome thanked Jean and told him to wait there a second while she went into the back. She returned a few moments later, changed into a pair of dungarees and a navy blue shirt. She invited Jean in for a bite to eat as a reward for bringing back her pocketbook with all of its contents intact. She also told him her mother had gone to church and wouldn't be returning before six that evening. She told Jean to have a seat while she turned the fire down on the Sunday dinner she was preparing.

"Thank you very much. I hope some of my home cooked roast beef smothered in onions will be enough to repay you for all the help you've done for me the last twenty-four hours, Mister..."

"Jean Paul," he said, finishing her sentence in his most suave, debonair tone.

"Jean Paul? I never heard that name before...What kind of name is that?" probed Winsome. She had turned off the fires and the house was filled with the smell of the food she'd cooked. It was an aroma as scintillating as her perfume had been the night he'd first seen her.

"It's a French name," Jean said proudly. "I was born in Haiti. Everyone here calls me John, but that's my birth name."

Winsome stared at him in disbelief then crossed her arms over her chest and asked, "So how is it you sound as if you is a true yardy?"

Jean laughed at his petite interrogator. "Well, my father is from Haiti and my mother come from Jamaica. She from country, over in Wakefield. So, I guess you could say mi really and truly a Jaitian."

She shook her head, looking totally confused. "Jaitian? How you mean a Jaitian?"

Jean looked concerned. He put a hand on her shoulder as though he'd just heard she'd caught some dread disease. "Don't tell me you've never heard of Jaitians before!"

Winsome shook her head. "No. I'm sorry. I never. What's that?"

"A Jamaican Haitian, silly!" Jean answered playfully.

She rolled her eyes at his corny joke but had to laugh in spite of herself.

Jean's mouth began to water when he saw the plate she had prepared for him. The white platter held roast beef, cabbage, rice, peas and carrots, all picture perfect. She sat at the table and began to eat nonchalantly. He ate slowly, not wanting the absolutely delectable meal to end, making small talk with her about her house and the neighborhood.

Neither of them mentioned what had happened the night before. He didn't want to make her think of Dexter and she was too embarrassed by what the jerk had done to want to discuss it. They kept the conversation, light and civil. Even though they were relatively strangers, they both felt comfortable around each other. They were comfortable enough that, once he was done eating, Jean asked, "How you get that coolie looking hair deh?"

She ran her hands through it, as if to make sure it was still there and Jean realized that her hair was the farthest thing from her mind. A lot of women with her grade hair acted conceited and superior because they attached importance to it but she wasn't that type. She explained to Jean that her father's side of the family came from a rebel tribe of slaves called the Maroons. They had escaped from slavery into the wilds of the Jamaican bush where no white man would dare come for them and settled in the mountainous lands. They would raid British slave outposts and kill whites who came in pursuit of them. They were the Original founders of Old Town and New Town. She went on to explain that on her mother's side descended from the Arawak Indians who, along with the Caribs, were the original inhabitants of Jamaica.

Jean liked the fact that such a beautiful woman knew her history and had a sense of knowledge of herself. She wasn't shallow and pretentious like most of the good looking women he had dealt with before. He was feeling more content by the minute with her and he felt obligated to elaborate on his family's history as well.

He explained how his great grandfather, twice removed, had fought in the effort to free Haiti from France way back in 1804. They also had Arawak in common, because his grandmother on his mother's side had Arawak blood in her too.

They sat in Winsome's house talking for hours about their history. Time had passed effortlessly and Winsome suddenly realized how long it had been since she had an intelligent conversation. She was about to tell him so when the phone rang.

She excused herself and answered it. Jean watched as her face changed, reddening and becoming a perfect mask of anger. "No! No! And don't you ever call me again!" She said furiously before slamming the handset back into its receiver.

The spell had been broken. The Winsome who stalked back to the table was not the same happy, intellectual young woman who'd left it.

"That was Dexter!" She said furiously.

"You mean the id-i-ot bwoy who started all that mess last night?"

"True, that id-i-ot deh!" She laughed without mirth smiling revealing her pure ivory toned teeth and started prompting Jean to the door. She thanked Jean for bringing back her purse and he thanked her for the delicious food but it was time for him to leave as her mother would be coming home soon and she wouldn't take too kindly to finding a strange man being in her home when she came back from church.

Jean asked Winsome when he would see her again, slightly pressing, eager to spend more time in her presence. Winsome said she'd just broke up with her boyfriend and wasn't sure when she would need male company again. Jean felt elated that Winsome now spoke of Dexter in the past tense and that she had made it clear to him that they were no longer an item. He actually got a small kick out of being there to hear her break the news to Dexter as well.

"I hear you," he responded, "but you can come to Papine down town anytime when you ready fi see me again. You nah affi make no promises, just come through so we can discuss some possibilities, seen? I work there six days of the week, all day long..."

She smiled. "Mi nah go make no promise...but we'll see what can happen."

Three weeks later, Jean was at his normal post in Papine, where he'd encountered the short balding American tourist.

"Hello, my friend," The fat man said joyously, "How are you?"

Jean couldn't complain and he told the tourist as much. "But what are you doing here, still? I thought you'd left weeks ago or was it that Jamaica is so nice you had to come back twice?" Jean asked.

"No, I been here the whole time. I went from Kingston to Negril and then to Ocho Rios. We stayed about a week in each town. My wife and I leave for New York tomorrow, as a matter of fact."

Jean smiled broadly and the man returned the smile with an even bigger one of his own. He looked good, well rested, fed and relaxed. His vacation had been good to him. The time he'd spent in Jamaica had probably extended his life by a decade.

"I want to thank you again. I can't begin to tell you how many people tried to take advantage of me while I was here," he said good naturedly. "If it hadn't been for you telling me about the exchange rate so soon, I would have lost thousands of dollars." He removed a pen from his pocket and a flyer.

He ripped a small piece of paper off and began to write cautiously. "My name is Judge Raymond Blackwell. If you ever come to The States, young man, don't hesitate to call me anytime."

Jean shook hands with him and looked for a token to give his friend in appreciation. He found it, a sculpture of the Lady of the Sea, the intricate waves carved scroll like at her feet. Jean removed it and heard the tourist catch his breath. He held the sculpture towards the man and carefully, softly the tourist took it in hand. He reached for his wallet but Jean would not allow it. The man's wife had been his muse for that piece and though he had never expected to see him again, it seemed only right for him to have it.

He started to leave and Jean turned to watch him go. Behind him, a voice queried, "How much is that piece in the front?" Before Jean turned back around. Even before he had a chance to remember how badly he'd hoped for her to come and how close he'd come to losing hope after so long. He knew just exactly who it was.

He turned to greet Winsome and the judge used that instant to slip a bill into his shirt pocket with a hearty pat. "Son, don't ever sell yourself cheap. Buy some more wood, some more inks, and make some more masterpieces for me to buy when I return next year." He said, laughing as he walked away.

Jean dug the bill out of his pocket and shook his head, whistling when he saw the denomination. The judge had money to burn, Jean found himself thinking.

He turned his attention back to Winsome and she gave him a playful smile. "Oh well, hello to you too. Mr. Jean Paul, is this how you gonna treat me...you tell me say come and visit you when I'm ready. Then I visit you and you a gwaan as if you nah waan see me. I bet you actin like that, because your girlfriend somewhere around, isn't she?" Winsome asked slyly.

Her age showed and Jean could see how young and vibrant the twenty one year old beauty truly was. Her brown skin was smooth and clear, her eyes aglow with mischief and humor.

He gave her an innocent look. "No, no, love its nothing like that. You caught me off guard, is all..."

She kept her face stern. "What's the matter with you mon? I asked how much is the piece right there." Jean's eyes traveled to where she was pointing only to follow them up to the sky. She laughed. "No, I'm just kidding. I was in the area and I wanted to pay you a little visit. So, this is what you do in Papine..." She looked around at all of his pieces, pausing sometimes to stare at things she found particularly striking.

Jean's art was truly beautiful and it was hard to not be engrossed by his talent. He had a way of bringing life to paint and paper, wood and metal that took her breath away. She was truly in awe. "This is nice." She said at ·last.

Jean was flattered. He took his talents for granted but he was always moved by people who had strong reactions to his work. He couldn't suppress his smile but he tried to make his tone casual. "Yeah, now you know what I do and where I work... What is it that you do? You some kind of nurse or something?"

She was wearing all white, a severe high necked dress, thick stockings and even white clogs. Oddly enough, she still looked good. Her nubile body was still shapely in the drab costume and the ghastly color shrouding them couldn't disguise the perfect bow of her legs.

"I work down the road on Main street, at the Humming Bird Hotel."

It made sense. The tourist attractions and hotels only hired pretty women.

Jean cracked a smile. "Really? Because my next guess, outside of you being a nurse, would have been that you were an angel and you are being missed in heaven right now. Maybe I can have you for my angel and my night nurse one day still?"

She rolled her eyes and tried to give him a screw face but couldn't help herself and began laughing instead.

Over the next few weeks, Winsome would come by Papine to check on Jean. First, she did this a few times a week. Then, gradually, she began coming by everyday until she became a regular bright spot in his day and he began to expect her. Their friendship blossomed so beautifully and smoothly that Jean feared Winsome might not want more than that. She was comfortable with him and the average man would have been all over her trying to make advances since two months had passed since her breakup with Dexter. But, he wasn't average and would never want to do the ordinary. Jean's plan was to play things casually and make her sweat awhile before he asked her to let things take their due course romantically.

She came to see him, all that time, because her mother was strict and would be extra critical about her bringing home another so soon after Dexter, so she hesitated about asking him to her home. But, one day, out of the blue, she invited him to dinner again. And, she made it sound as if she were daring him, slipping it in while she talked about her irresistible cooking.

Her eyes looked like she had been thinking and Jean knew without her saying so that this was not a casual invitation. He accepted nonchalantly but, inside, he was ecstatic. They made plans to go out to the cinema that weekend and Jean gave her a lingering look as she left, letting her see his interest plainly. She smiled back and looked away, refusing to boldly show him how she felt.

That night, he searched for and found a beautiful piece of mahogany that he had been saving in a closet. He began skillfully chipping away at the wood, letting himself envision the completed piece. He worked from his soul and his hands were like magic, carving and sanding until there was now a masterpiece in place of what was a simple piece of wood. He was at work all night and, as the dawn crested through his window, he realized that he hadn't slept at all but didn't feel tired.

He didn't tell Winsome about the piece the next day. That night, he painted it with the utmost care, highlighting and defining every detail. The next morning again, he greeted the dawn without having slept a wink. The paint had dried and he wrapped the piece carefully, setting it apart from his other pieces.

The next week, they went to downtown Kingston for their date. They walked around the shops, talking and getting to know one another, taking in the beautiful sights. They went to the movies and saw an imported karate feature. They both enjoyed it immensely and Winsome was delighted to find she could be silly and playful with Jean. Dexter had taken himself far too seriously to play around.

He would have cursed her for being foolish if she had tried to do the moves she'd seen in the movie in front of him. She felt like she'd been born again, like she'd been given a second chance at life. Jean was like a breath of fresh air, cool water. He refreshed her and made her feel happier than she'd felt since she was a child.

The weekends became her salvation. She worked hard all week, stole precious moments with him during the day but couldn't let her hair down and have fun until the weekends. They went everywhere, it seemed, and talked about everything. Jean was the perfect gentleman. He wasn't phony or putting on a facade. He was genuinely a good man. She had given him hugs and kisses on the cheek and he never pressured her beyond that. She knew he had feelings for her and she admired how he could still manage to enjoy the slow pace of their friendship without pressing her. His playing the background turned her on more than the average man would have. She was ready for the next step.

In her heart, she was an old fashioned girl and she could never be with a man her mother didn't give approval of. Her mother wasn't stuck up, in Winsome's view. However, she did have standards for the men who wanted to court her daughters and she made no bones about expressing her feelings. Her mouth didn't stay shut when it came to those who didn't measure up but Winsome knew Jean would pass any test.

Jean was so excited to meet Winsome's mother because he knew what she thought of him could go a long way with Winsome and possibly make or break their relationship. He'd practiced being on his best behavior and his table manners the whole week before he came to Sunday dinner. The anticipation was killing him and he felt his heart racing faster and faster every time he pictured his sweet Winsome as the day drew nearer.

Finally the day came and, at six thirty Jean found himself outside of Winsome's door. He rang the bell and, after a moment, Winsome came to it and opened it for him, giving him a warm embrace. Then she sat him in a seat that faced the street and told him her mother was in the back changing from her church clothes. She teased him about the caliber of meal she'd prepared, boasting on her culinary skill as he shot back barbs, playing with her too. She'd killed off his anxiety within ten minutes of his arrival and he was actually laughing and enjoying himself while they waited for her mother.

In Jamaica, it's customary to have certain meals on certain days and, as it was, Sunday dinner at the Stuarts was roast beef. Winsome had arranged gigantic serving platters of rice, roast beef and vegetables on the table, as well as a pitcher of homemade lemonade. The food looked and smelled delicious and Jean literally found his mouth watering. After a moment, she seated him at the table across from where she would sit.

Winsome had set out a beautiful place setting at the head of the table for her mother. She warned him not to touch anything and not to have any bites of food until she returned. Then, laughing, she went to get her mother.

The woman looked exactly like Winsome except that her hair was gray and black and she was hunched over, walking slowly as she held the young lady's arm for support. Once they reached the table, Jean stood and pulled out her chair. She was seated and Winsome touched him lightly on the chest, as they stood facing her. "Mama, this is John. John, this is my mother, Mrs. Stuart."

The lady gave him a dry smile as she appraised him. Her face was still, not frowning or smiling, giving no indication of what she thought of him. Just taking in the details. "Oh, so you is the young man my daughters been telling me about for weeks now. I see why she keep talking about you. You are very handsome." She said flatly and waited for his response.

Jean couldn't think of one. It would have been phony to tell her she was beautiful or some such thing so instead he simply nodded and smiled. After a moment, she did too. "Winsome tells me you work with paintings and wood sculptures." She began as she poured herself a glass of lemonade. Winsome moved to do it for her but she shooed her away, indicating for her to take her seat instead. "I always love a man who can work him wood!" She finished with an impish ear-to-ear grin.

"Mama!" Winsome screamed in embarrassment.

"I'm sorry, but it's true...if I didn't like the way your father worked his wood, you wouldn't be here right now." The older woman said with a wink.

Winsome shrieked and grimaced, mortified. She ladled food onto her plate and began stuffing her mouth full, knowing there was nothing she could do. She let her mother have the floor.

"So where ya come from, John?"

Mrs. Stuart passed him a serving bowl, filled to the top with a steaming mound of sweet white rice. Jean took the bowl, unaware until then that rice even had a smell. He began to help himself as he answered her. "Well, I'm a country boy from Wakefield. I moved to Kingston about two years ago."

Mrs. Stuart was an old fashioned woman and she liked to see a man eat. Displeased with the polite amount Jean had given himself. She reached and took the bowl from him, ladling out a man sized portion. Jean smiled and let her finish, pleased that he was saved from embarrassment. Because, the truth was, if the food tasted as good as it looked, he was ready to eat the whole table by himself! "So you come from country," she said as she served, "I like people from the country. They know what it mean to work hard for their living and make it. You come from country to make it in the big city, eh?" She smiled. "That's good, that's good...We have some family in the country, in Saint Ann you know. Did Winsome tell you?"

He shook his head, smileing looking over at Winsome. She was nervous, he could tell and that made him smile. She wanted her mother to like him.

"Yeah mon, we have some family in Westmoreland and Saint Ann Our family owned land out there for years," she said, expressively. Jean noted that she was very proud of her family. "So country boy, where you sell your goods?" Mrs. Stuart asked knowingly and Jean realized that there was more to this woman than met the eye. She hadn't always been well off and she'd learn to respect her roots and the path that had brought her there. He could only admire that.

"I sell down town in Papine, from Monday to Saturday. Sunday is the only day I take off."

She smiled again. "That's good, that's good! A hard worker, with your own business at a young age. I need a hard working bwoy for my daughter." Winsome looked up at her unable to speak when she heard that and Ms. Stuart winked at Jean again, enjoying the way she had put her daughter on the spot. "My late husband Roy was a hard worker. He died a few years back from whatever the hell chemicals they use at that damn bauxite mine or so the doctor dem say…" Jean touched her hand to comfort her. She had loved the man and it was still painful to talk about him. Jean could see the pain on her face and he couldn't do much more than that. She held his hand then she looked into his eyes.

She looked long, really seeing what was there and not whatever character he might be playing. She was a good judge of people and she inspected him carefully, not missing a beat. Finally, without smiling she said to Winsome in a flat tone. "I like this young man already. He knows what it feels like to earn a living from a hard day's labor. I like him. More than that big headed spoiled son of a bitch you used to keep friends with." She said without laughter, looking directly at her daughter allmost af if she was looking through her.

Mrs. Stuart had tolerated Dexter because of circumstances beyond her control. Winsome thought her mother had liked the boy but honestly, she had to admit that wasn't the truth. Mrs. Stuart had been polite and tolerant but she had never smiled or laughed with Dexter or tried to engage him in a conversation. Dexter had been syrupy sweet to her, buying her flowers and kissing her hand whenever he came there but Winsome could see now that her mother had not been fooled. Winsome couldn't ever quite put her finger on it,but there seemed to be a spacific reason why her mother never cared for Dexter.

"John, it brings me the greatest joy one can receive on the face of the Earth to see my daughters happy… after their father died, tis dem alone that take care of me and keep me content…"

Winsome felt a warm sensation in her belly that went all the way up to her throat until she was almost choking. Jean looked back and forth between the two of them and then went back to eating his meal, aware that he had been part of an especially heartfelt moment. He was usually uneasy around his friends mothers but he felt comfortable with Winsome's. He felt like in time, she could possibly be as close to him as family.

"John," Mrs. Stuart said after she and Winsome cleared off the table, "come over here for a second so an old lady can get a better look at you. I wanna see your hands." Jean thought it was an odd request but he shrugged and went over to her, holding out his hands. "Don't be scared now bwoy, I'm not gon' put a obia hex on you!" She said with a chuckle as she felt the inside of Jean's palm with her finger tips.

Jean watched her and waited for a verdict, wondering if she read palms or believed in signs. "No dear, its nothing," she explained, laughing. "Mi nah mean no harm. I just couldn't believe that such a handsome man work with his hands but, by the roughness of your hand, I see you are a hard worker. Sit back down, young man." Jean tried to do what she'd done, looking at his own hands but not seeing anything. His hands were such a part of him that he couldn't tell whether they were rough or not.

To Winsome, she made a face and said, "Winnie, I'm done. You can take me back fi mi room and let this old woman rest her vexed bones."

The young girl waved off her ridiculousness at calling herself old. In Winsome's eyes, Mrs. Stuart was as firm and fit as most women half her age. The grief and loss of her husband had weighted down on her but she was still healthy and strong. The young woman did not see her mother as others might have seen her, white haired, front teeth missing, gaps and all.

Mrs. Stuart smiled at Jean and said in parting, "John, take care of mi Winsome…I like you bwoy but, if you hurt her feelings, I'll find you, and bite you to death."

They all laughed and Winsome shook her head, hurrying to get her mother back to her room before she could do anything else to embarrass her.

When she returned, they settled into the couch in the living room to watch the television. Jean couldn't help but notice all of the nice things in her home and all the amenities that some people could scarcely dream of. He took it all in, the furniture, the silk curtains, the telephone on the ornately carved King Louis table and the floor model TV.

Winsome saw him looking and he finally broke down and asked her. "I don't want to be nosy… but how is it your family has such nice things? You rich or something?"

True, they did live in a nice part of town and her home was one of the nicest on Red Hills Road but Jean was certain that even the other people living next door didn't have all of the nice things the Stuarts did.

"You mad or something, man?" Winsome asked him in response. "We nah rich…just all right. When my father died, the company he worked for set up a fund for my mother. He worked there for years and he was well liked by everybody. Besides, my sister work in New York and she send us American money and I work at the hotel. So, with all the different money comin', we do all right. We nah go get rich and switch…yet."

Jean was satisfied with that. It had occurred to him that maybe Dexter had bought all of these things; in which case, Jean wasn't sure he wouldn't have got up and left. That not being the case, he changed the subject and got back to his master plan of winning her heart. "Yeah, I hear dat…now if only I could get you to like me as much as your momma, then I'd be in good shape still."

Winsome swatted at his arm, like he was foolish but slid closer on the couch and cuddled against him. "True, momma like you, ya know? She say she like you a whole heap better than my other boyfriend because you work for your own money and you know how to talk to people. She said Dex was antisocial, conceited. My momma's something else. Once you get to know her, she'll have you laughing for days."

That wasn't good enough. He didn't want to be running a race with Dexter or anybody else for that matter. "So, that's how the two a we a go stay now? I'm your boyfriend?" His tone was serious and he stared at her with a raised brow.

Winsome didn't understand what had offended him. "I like you enough to come see you everyday...I introduced you to my momma...we go out on dates...I really like you, John. You can be my boyfriend...if you want to."

That didn't change the look on his face and Winsome felt even more confused. He shook his head, his eyes never leaving hers. "I appreciate the offer, seen? But, I can't be your boyfriend!"

Winsome had never felt so embarrassed in her life! She felt like she would drop dead on the spot from the embarrassment of having thrown herself at him and then being rejected. She had never been turned down by any man for any reason but it hurt more so coming from a man she was so attracted to. The man she knew who was to be her destiny. She covered her face in her hands.

"I can't be your boyfriend," Jean continued, "because I am a man and I don't deal with no little girls. If I deal with you from this point on you is my woman. A boyfriend wouldn't know how to treat such a empress like you. "

They kissed. His mouth met hers urgently, hurriedly, hungrily and passionately. All of the subtle hints and leading gestures they'd made towards each other over the weeks melted away into the blending of their souls and they were at a place both of them knew they belonged. The awesome connection they made between one another was more than just mundane. It felt spiritial, and metaphysical for the both of them. For a long while, as his hands caressed her body and their tongues coiled around one another, they let their hands, mouths and eyes do all of the talking for them.

When Jean broke away from Winsome's grip, she felt an eagerness that she had never felt before. She wanted to make love to him and needed to feel him deep within her from his mere touch alone. Something that had never happened to her, not even when Dexter was at his best sexually. eventhough Dexter was the only man she'd ever given her self to.

He had to go, he had a friend waiting. She wanted to beg him to stay, offer him something he would really like, if he did but she knew it was way too soon. She kissed him once more, letting him taste her tongue. As he walked away, she felt the burning ache, and desire to see him again. Her whole body was tingling from his touch and she felt like her center was ingulfed in flames.

CHAPTER FOUR

China waited casually in front of the house, amusing himself with an old soccer ball he'd found. As Jean got the dominos and so they could set up the regular Sunday game. Which consisted of drinking beers and puffing some good herb from Chinaman's stash. Usually, Jean would talk trash boldly, nonstop set after set but this game found him pensive. China watched his friend and then commented on it. Jean mumbled that everything was cool but China laughed. "Bullshit! Dat gal Winsome got your nose open. Give me all the details. What happened at she house that have you sitting here like this?"

Jean dismissed him with a wave. "Everything crisp! I met her momma, and she momma like me and she like me."

China wouldn't relinquish the teasing. "Oh yeah. Cool. I'm gonna have to get you a whole heap of gals you like, so I can win without you saying I cheated every time we play."

For Jean, that confirmed he was indeed a cheater and that he could never beat him otherwise.

"So how long till you give she the peg and move on to the next victim?" China asked passing him the spliff.

Jean took it and shook his head as though he pitied his friend. "Nah mon, ya nah get it? Winsome is my woman now and I'm thinking of what mi a go do with the rest of the gals dem."

China understood the words but he couldn't grasp what his friend was saying. Jean was a committed bachelor and China couldn't conceive of him picking one girl and being with her only. "A me Chinaman, you know? Who ya think ya talkin' to? I know after you had her in bed, you'll send her on her way and keep doing to these women what it is that we do to them." He had his palm up, waiting for Jean to give him dap on what he'd just said.

Jean looked at his hand and didn't give him anything. Chinaman looked at him in shock, his mouth open and head tilted to the side. "Nah, mon, you nah understand. I like this girl. Really. She's different from any other woman I ever met. I remember my momma telling me that if you ever meet a girl like that. You should hold on to her because you may never find someone like that again!"

China shook his head, glad it wasn't him. He loved woman too much to pick just one. "If you're gonna get serious about somebody," he started, unconvinced "I guess Winsome is as good as anybody to get serious with. She come from a decent home and like I say, she a nice girl. It might could work , ya know. I don't think Dexter would care…"

Jean slammed down his last domino, the winner of that set. "My youth. Why the fuck you keep chatting about the bwoy Dexter? Didn't you just hear me tell you Winsome is my woman now? Mi nah care bout a little punk that would beat his woman in public and make a scene like he did."

China didn't care in the slightest that his friend was vexed. It was up to him to keep things in perspective. "True, I agree with you Dexter was acting like a punk that night... Matter of fact, Dexter really is a punk, but he still can have you hurt badly."

Jean wouldn't see reason. "How you mean he a punk but can hurt me still? That doesn't make sense. Bredren make sense when you talk to me!" Jean emphatically stated.

China took a long pull, carefully blowing smoke away from Jean but still watching him. After a moment, he said, "What I mean is Dexter never really had to fight his own fight. He never had to struggle like the rest a we because of who his father is. His father is a real bad mon from years gone, and he has people guarding Dexter everywhere he go. His father is a don."

The seriousness of that wasn't lost on Jean. He understood the weight that the word of a don carried and how many people he could count as loyal henchmen who might not have respected Dexter but had learned to fear his father. Jean didn't say it to Chinaman but, in his heart he knew, he would never back down from Dexter. He could have the whole island with him and his father holding his hand and Jean would never run from any challenge either of them. Jean didn't answer and China let the matter drop, satisfied that he had done all he could.

The next weekend Jean arrived at Winsome's house with a picnic basket and a bottle of wine. He was dressed to the nines. His tan button up shirt was matched with black slacks and brown suede British shoes. After his steaming shower, he'd doused himself in what the ladies claimed was an irresistible cologne and he'd gotten a fresh hair cut.

Looking and smelling like a million bucks, he rang the bell. Winsome must have read his mind. When she opened the door, she nearly took his breath away. She was wearing a beige two piece outfit. The shirt was form fitting showing a little of her flat mid riff and the skirt fell sensuously against her legs right below her knees. She wore black sandals and a bright, ripe red rose in her hair. She wore her jewels and the play of the gold against her delectable caramel skin set off the outfit to perfection.

Hand in hand, the young lovers strolled along, on their first outing as an official couple. Heads turned as they made their way to Conscious Spring Road, where they'd decided to catch the bus.

"So, where is my man taking me today?" Winsome asked when they'd arrived. The bus wouldn't be there for a while and she used her hands to shade her eyes from the blazing sun.

Jean smiled mischievously, "Just gwaan easy now gal. I've got nothing but good intentions for you..." He said lecherously and the two shared a laugh.

"I hear dat, but my daddy used to say the road to hell is paved with good intentions." Winsome shot back.

Jean waxed philosophical. "I've traveled many a road in my life, but never has one of those roads led me to hell. I thought since I was with my angel, surely, I must be on my way to heaven!"

She knew it was just a sweet nothing but she couldn't help but take the bait. She gushed, holding his arm tightly as she pulled him closer.

They boarded the bus and went downtown, enjoying rum raisin ice cream and patties from the patty shop. Winsome was bored soon. She hated run of the mill dates and she was hoping Jean would take her somewhere exciting instead. She was just about to voice her disappointment when she noticed he'd steered her to the bus headed outside of Kingston.

He wouldn't answer any questions of where he was taking her, no matter how she tried. She talked to him sweetly, curtly and, at one point, even joked that she was afraid of where they'd end up. However, he was silent until about 45 minutes later when they arrived at the ruins of Port Royal . A city that was a central trading post in the Caribbean for the British Empire. It was also considered to be the Sodom and Gomorrah of it's time due to its loose morals and rampant fornication. Just as Sodom and Gomorrah met a horrific end, Port Royal mirrored it in its tragedy. It was completely destroyed by an earthquake in the latter part in the 17th Century.

It was stunningly beautiful. The old castle had been built in the 15 Century by the Spanish. It had been used as a fort and the remnants of cannons and fortifications remained. It was rumored that the famed pirate Henry Morgan, a.k.a Red Beard, had fought Christopher Columbus in a battle there. He'd defeated the conquistador and sent him packing out to sea in a small row boat. Throwing out well over five hundred pounds of gold over the side of his ship along his way out to the ocean. Glimmers of gold were aplenty on the breathtaking beach, feeding the rumors. The main fort in Port Royal was a castle that stood over a ledge above the sea where you could stand and salute the emerald green water crashing against the jagged rocks some forty feet below.

Jean held her hand as they ascended. And, when they reached the top, he held her in his arms as she surveyed the beauty all around them, feeling like the luckiest woman in the whole world. She couldn't say how long they were there. She felt like she could have stayed forever, listening to the rhythm of the water and breathing in the crisp clean air of the sea breeze.

Jean took her by the hand and led her down the stairs to the beach. They walked along the shores until they reached a deserted crevice and Jean put down the blanket. It was their own private spot, too far from the castle for anyone to see them and Winsome felt that she was not only the luckiest woman in the world but maybe even the only woman in the world. It was as if only they existed, there drinking wine and listening to the crash of the surf.

Jean reached into the picnic basket and came out with a neatly wrapped package. He handed it to Winsome and smiling gleefully, she tore the wrapping off like a child with a present. It was the beautiful mahogany piece Jean had made several weeks earlier.

She stared at it dumbstruck for a long while. It was a likeness of her. He had captured all of her features precisely and dressed her in full Arawak ensemble. Above the mahogany, Winsome's head was a multicolored headdress, intricately sculpted and painted with excruciating detail. Her body was garbed in the ceremonial clothing of a queen and the figures arms were outstretched.

Winsome had never, received a present this special. No one had ever put as much time and energy into something made just for her as Jean had done. She was more than flattered, she was honored. She kissed his cheek and held the precious sculpture in her hands, stroking and examining it.

"I may not be rich, or have a lot of fancy things but I can still give you all of me." Jean whispered into her ear.

She kissed him again, fully this time.

Winsome began to kiss Jean with more passion than she had ever experienced before in her entire life. As Winsome kissed Jean, his hands began exploring her body while maneuvering her until she lay next to him. While still fondling and kissing Winsome, Jean pushed away the picnic basket with his leg as to make more room for them on the pallet.

As Winsome lay on the blanket, Jean rose above her, bobbling on his knees. He began to slowly and dramatically unbutton his shirt and reveal his chiseled torso. Then, he took the shirt all the way off and started kissing Winsome again. Only this time, he began palming her breast under her shirt. A few minutes later, Jean totally pulled her shirt away and unfastened her bra from the back, revealing Winsome's perfect bountiful bare D cup breasts. Jean had imagined how her breasts would look but, once he really saw them, he couldn't believe that they looked better than he could ever envision.

He took a second look at them and marveled at how perky they were, even with Winsome laying down, and he had to have a mouthful. He opened his mouth and put Winsome's left nipple into it along with most of her perfectly shaped brown areola. Winsome quivered with pleasure just from the warmth of Jean's breath before he even began to suckle her chest. Jean felt her nipples enlarge on his tounge and harden in his mouth. As he kept at her chest, he also simultaneously went up her dress and began to rub the inside of her upper right thigh as he lay on top of her.

A few minutes later, Jean moved his hand between her legs. He caressed the outer lining of her panties, dead in the middle of them finding Winsome's pleasure button. All the while still suckling her chest. After toying with Winsome's button for a while, Jean could feel actual heat coming from between her legs. He slowly and seductively eased up from on top of Winsome, then bent over and began removing her drenched white French cut satin panties.

Jean's hand found it's way back in between Winsome's thighs where her panties were a few moments before. Only Jean's fingers now found their way into her wet spot again…and again…and again. Winsome's eyes rolled in the back of her head and her neck went limp while she moaned in pure ecstasy.

Winsome let out a rumbling groan that turned into an intoxicating gasp. Then, her whole body began to shudder into an uncontrollable involentary convulsion causeing her thighs to quake as she released a bitter sweet nectar from her forbidden fruit. Jean couldn't stand it any longer. The moment he had been waiting for since he first saw her in the dancehall had finally arrived. He gently kissed her on her neck and stood up to take off the rest of his clothes. Then Winsome took off her dress as well as her slip. They both lay back down with Jean on top of Winsome, open mouth kissing her repeatedly as they were now skin to skin together as one. He positioned himself and leaned his waist in between her smooth caramel nubile thighs. With several thrusts and a small struggle, Jean entered Winsome's sweet, snug ,and very moist utopia. He gave her long smooth strokes making sure to give his best performance to please her more than he pleasured himself. So he would leave the best possible impression on his new lover. He was in rare form doing an excellent job, causing her to grimace her face as tears of ecstasy fell from the corner of her eyes into the casum of her ears. She was biting her bottom lip from the pretty pain he was thoroughly executing.

Winsome, all the while calling out Jean's name, was panting heavily and moaning with every powerful trust. To Jean's ears, it sounded like a sweet symphony of seduction. Winsome rocked her hips in a circular rhythm which allowed her to meet his every stroke as she was thoroughly enjoying slowly milking the sweet venom from every inch of Jean's serpent. Then suddenly Jean began to slow his pace, tense up and his abdominals began to flex as he let out a short and sparatic series of intense grunts. Causing Winsome to dig her nails deep into Jean's back ,and pull him tightly into her.

At that very moment Winsome felt a warm sensation from deep with in. She felt an intense tingle that shot from the base of her spine to the top of her head all the way down to her finger tips and her toes. All at once there was a calm numbing sensation that washed over her body and spirit. She'd totally given into Jean's will ,and was completly his now. Every part of her being belonged to him, her mind, body, and soul. She was now his earth ,and he controlled all the elements that comprised her very existance includeing her wind,and fire. Jean could make her rain at will. What just happened felt so good Winsome wanted to scream, however she was out of breath.

In a little over two hours, they managed to twists their bodies into at least ten positions, right there on the beach at Port Royal. The fact that they were outside, and someone may have caught them in the act, turned them on even more. Jean had taken Winsome to heights of pleasure that she couldn't have imagined was humanly possible. The fire works they generated were easily brighter than New Year's Eve and the Fourth of July combined.

After they made love, sensuously and passionately on the beach. Winsome realized that she hadn't ever known that loving could be so good. Nothing that she had ever done or had done to her touched the beauty of what she experienced with Jean. It wasn't just making her feel as though the Earth had quaked six times on that beach. It wasn't that he was sweet and had made that beautiful sculpture of her. It wasn't his good looks and his chiseled perfect body, either. It wasn't even the fact that he was head and shoulders above Dexter in every category. It was that Winsome knew she'd found her soul mate. Winsome's heart was like a house of love waiting to be properly built and her emotions were the material and fabric to build her house from the ground up. The only man that she'd given her heart to thus far had broken it in two. However it seemed as though Jean would be her master builder who would turn the driftwood shanty of her heart into an impenetrable fortress.

After their marathon love making they fell fast asleep on the beach. His body covering hers at first and then wrapped in the blanket snuggled together. Until the waves lapped at their feet and they had to scurry away their clothing and possessions before the in coming tide drenched everything. When they'd woke, it wasn't quite dusk yet. The sun was low in the sky but fierce still and they played like children in its amber glow. They frolicked nude in the shallow waters of the beach, washing the sand from each other's bodies. Then, Jean lay back and floated in the tide, letting the sun kiss him, feeling like he was in paradise.

He got her back home around nine. At her door, they couldn't bear to part. Jean kept saying he was leaving and Winsome kept acknowledging he had to go but they couldn't stop kissing and holding each other and talking about everything that occurred that day. After what happened in Port Royal, Winsome was smitten with Jean. Just the smell of him made the hair on the back of her neck stand up and turned her blood into sweet wine. Winsome still held the statue he'd carved, like a trophy of some sort. People stared at it all the way from the beach through Kingston and back to her home. She'd proudly told anyone who'd asked that her man, the phenomenal artist, made it for her and that it was the closest thing to her heart while she would treasure it always...

CHAPTER FIVE

Several months had passed since Jean and Winsome were together and it was now the latter part of February. With each new day that passed, the bond between them grew stronger and the unconditional love they had for one another was unparalleled. They spent so much of their free time together that, after awhile, Winsome found she was unconsciously mimicking Jean's body language and some of the phrases he used. They were truly happy with one another and Jean's feeling of being an outsider was all but nonexistent when he was with Winsome. She made him proud to be her man.

Things were going good for Jean on a financial level as well. With so many tourists pouring into Papine market, Jean was able to stash away a nice amount of money even with his increased payments to Bigga.

Everything was fine until one day when Chinaman's friend couldn't make their usual Sunday soccer match and China needed a man to take his place. Jean was a natural athlete and China asked him to be a stand in. They were scheduled to play Dexter's team but China didn't think it would be a big deal. Jean and Winsome had already been together for six months and Dexter had been seen around town with one beauty after another so the loss of Winsome didn't appear to be bothering him one bit. The games were competitive and as both teams were regarded as tied for the title of "best". China didn't think Dexter would pay Jean any close attention.

The two teams met up a few miles on the outskirts of Kingston on Spanish Town Road at about three in the afternoon. Jean had bought Winsome to the game and she sat apart from the other spectators in the benches watching them, cheering her man on. Despite the laughter and conversation of the other spectators, Jean could hear her rooting "GO JOHN," enthusiastically, at the top of her lungs.

The two teams took the field and instantly, Jean took command of the ball. Within ten minutes of the game's start, he'd scored a goal. As soon as they got it back, Dexter's man sent the ball flying past China playing goalie, into their net. Quickly evening up the match and setting the stage for a contentious, intense game. They went hard at it for close to an hour and a half but, in the end, Chinaman's team was victorious.

They only won by one point but the game had been so action packed that the win was a big one. The heat that they'd played with melted away though, as the two teams shook hands and complimented each other on their excellent play. Just as Jean and Dexter came upon one another. Dexter extended his hand outward to Jean, and Winsome rushed the field and gave him a giant hug and kiss. Dexter's hand dropped and he screwed up his face in contempt for their union.

Noticing Dexter's rapid change of heart Jean asked, "So what's wrong bredren ya nah go shake my hand now?"

Dexter looked at Winsome, on whose face displayed a sense of contentment and sheer pleasure. She knew how jealous Dexter was and she delighted in the way the sight of the two of them together was eating him up.

"Nah mon," Dexter answered, never taking his eyes off her. "Or… at least not while that filthy whore is any where near my presence!"

There was laughter at this and Jean turned to see Rodrick and Marlon, two of Dexter's cousins and team members who were also on his security detail, cracking up.

"Well, I understand you're a sore loser and that's why you nuh waan fi shake mi hand but for your sake. I'll act like I didn't hear anything else." Jean said, directly challenging Dexter. Those that were on the field and heard the confrontation brewing moved away from Jean. They didn't know him that well and they feared what might happen after he'd said what he'd said and they didn't want to be in the crossfire.

China grabbed Jean by the shoulder and began pulling him away, realizing that it had been a mistake to bring him. Dexter shot back, behind them. "Pussy clot! You act as if you don't know who I am or what I could easy do to you. You should mind the way you speak to me, bwoy or you could find yourself in a whole heap of trouble." He let the threat hang there in the air, and his people began to file in behind him.

Jean shoved China off and faced him, furious. "Yeah mon, I hear of your rep. I hear that you is a big pussy who hide behind your men and can't fight. That's why I hear about you! That you is a pussy!" Jean stood alone, mimicking the way a cat meows after his last statement.

The danger in the air was real! Dexter's cousins were about to rush Jean and beat him into bloody unconsciousness when Dexter held them back and did something that surprised everyone there that day. "Joke, you a joke mon! I could beat you with one arm tied behind my back, you stinking Haitian! That's right! I know you is a Haitian. I know for a fact that no Haitian can beat any yard man. So, I'll give you one last chance to apologize before I beat you like you is a slave, all by myself. Oh, unless it is that you have enough heart to defend that slut bitch you with." He let a big smile cover his entire face almost before he took one last stab. "Then, we both can talk about how good my leftovers are!"

The men all looked at Winsome and she stared straight ahead, her profile sharp. Her eyes were furious and Jean threw his hands up to Dexter, resisting China. Who was still trying to get him to leave. They faced each other and squared off. In a flash, Dexter caught him on the side of his head with a round of punches. Some of them missed but his crew still cheered as he had thrown the first punch. He connected with Jean's head as Jean got low to bob and weave then caught him on the chin with a stiff left uppercut.

Jean was a tad bit dazed and he backed up a little. Dexter took that as a premature victory and his friends began cheering and throwing insults. When Dexter overzealously rushed in for the kill thinking Jean was ready to go down. Jean unleashed a volley of blows that caught Dexter at least half a dozen times in the mouth, face and head before he even knew what hit him.

Dexter got angry and delivered a right hook to the left side of Jean's jaw, slightly dazing him. He hit him in the eye with a right jab. Jean slowed down the onslaught by blocking the next flurry of punches he threw. Dexter became overconfident and dropped his guard.

Jean took two steps back and punched Dexter with all of his might on the right side of his temple. Dexter felt the impact and staggered. His cousins started to rush Jean again but furious, Dexter held them off. He lunged wildly at Jean who hit him with a combination of two jabs to his eyes and a bolo to the throat. There was silence and, in that split second Dexter fell flat on his back where he stood. He was unconscious.

Two of his team mates tried to revive him. Dexter's cousins, Marlon and Rodrick, began running at top speed towards the car they came in. Jean stood there for a moment, savoring his victory until China pulled him by the arm to the other side of the field, where their friend Norville had his car. Everyone on the field had scattered and Jean suddenly realized that the other two were going to their cars to get guns.

They all barely squished into Norville's car when the rounds of semi-automatic gunfire lit up the afternoon. Marlon and Roderick were untrained but were firing so rapidly that they missed them by mere inches. They hit the bumper of Norville's car but he kept his head low and drove on, not stopping until they reached Jean's place in Kingston. The moment they went their separate ways, a chain of events was set off that would have a severe impact on the lives of everyone that was involved.

CHAPTER SIX

The whole scene felt surreal. China sat there shaking his head at his stupidity for bringing Jean and thinking nothing would happen. Winsome still bristled from the insults.However, she was so glad the second Jean dropped Dexter that she would have taken all the insults in the world to see that again. They all sat in his small flat reflecting on what happened. China ,and Jean were sitting at the table talking when they were interrupted by a loud, urgent sounding pounding at Jean's door. Everyone including Winsome stood at attention. Jean, still on edge after being shot at by Dexter's men, told Winsome and China to get back while he went to answer it. He stood along the doors side and asked in a deep voice, "Who is it?"

"My youth, it you want to live through the night, you'll open this blood clot door right ah now!" The reply came. Jean recognized the voice right away as Constable Brown but still hesitated to open for Bigga. He didn't know if Dexter wouldn't jump out from behind the fat black constable when he opened the door so he was leery. But, he couldn't dismiss the urgency of the man's tone.

"Hello good night, Constable Brown." He said when he opened the door at last.

"Fuck you chat bout, bwoy? Good night!!! You ah gwaan easy as if you nah know what happened over on Spanish Town Road! What is going through your mind, youth? I told you dat bwoy deh is don of his area and his father as well...you is fucken stupid? Dexter and his father are part of The Syndicate...they have a hit on you now bwoy. Twenty five thousand American dollars for the man who kill you. You got to leave Kingston, John, there's no other way. Now, pack your things. I'll be downstairs in the jeep, waiting for you!"

He said all this in one breath, not even waiting for Jean to acknowledge what he had said. There was no debating this, Jean realized.

"I won't leave you!" Winsome blurted out hurriedly and excited. Almost at the speed of sound, Jean began to pack his belongings into his large green duffel bag and instructed China to wait for him in the jeep with Bigga. Jean managed to pack a few changes of clothes and his whole life savings of about eight thousand American dollars. Which was a ransom in the street at that time in Jamaica. Only five minutes had passed, but Jean had finished packing everything he needed including his gun to make his get away and was in the back seat of Bigga's jeep with Winsome right by his side. Jean gave Bigga instructions on where to drop them off, and Bigga drove franticly like a mad man through the back streets of Kingston.

They reached Winsome's house about ten minutes later. With great urgency both Jean and Winsome jumped out and rushed into Winsome's house. Winsome burst through the door and discovered her mother in the living room watching the tele.

"Whah gwaan Winsome... Ah wah you a go do," Mrs. Stuart quizzed, noting the way she and Jean burst through the door.

"Momma mi affi pack some things so I can leave with Jean for a little while... he's gotta leave and I must go with him."

"What is you talkin bout gal... who is Jean and why do you have to leave with him?" Mrs. Stuart asked while scratching her head in a daze.

"Momma you know Jean. He's standing right deh so, I been with him for six months already!"

"No Winsome stay here... I'm not sure where I end up will be safe for you... but I promise as soon as everything dies down I'll be back for you... I promise!" Jean stated, striving to protect Winsome from his still unknown fate.

"Jean....this is Jean? Then why the hell you tell me the bwoy name is John then?"

"I told you that, because Jean is Haitian and I know how bad you talk about them and I know you wouldn't approve of me being with him!" Winsome responded.

"Gal you had a God damned Haitian in my house... They is filty people!!! I can't believe you would do such a thing. Why can't you stick to your own kind.... just why not your own kind," Winsome's mother said in a hysterical rant.

"Momma stop being ignorant! This is no time for one of your fits... besides Jean is my own kind... he's black, and I'm already two month's pregnant for him so, in a few months, you are going to have a Haitian grand baby. Your own flesh and blood you... are you gonna call your first born grand baby filthy too?" Winsome barked revealing for the first time to both Jean and her mother that she was bearing life.

At that moment, Mrs. Stuart collapsed into the chair she was sitting in before Jean and Winsome arrived. Her eyes rolled in her head as she cursed her daughter. As well as Jean and all Haitians in her deep native Jamaican country accent. It almost sounded as if she were speaking in tongues, she was so vehement. When she was done, she lay there collapsed, drained in almost a catatonic state. Winsome leaned over to try and revive her but a series of rapid and loud beeps from the horn of Bigga's jeep outside cut through the still of the night.

Her mother had made her decision and now Winsome made hers. There was nothing left to say and, with out any hesitation, Winsome walked out of the front door of her mother's house into the cool night without looking back.

They dropped China off at his apartment. He wasn't worried about beef or too concerned for his own safety. He only wanted to see Winsome and Jean off. He advised Jean to lie low for a few months, give the heat time to die down. He didn't have many words for Winsome but he gave her a hug and a blessing. Her decision to stick by Jean's side after her mother's disrespectful diatribe and rejection because of Jean's nationality filled him with a new reverence for her. She was loyal to her man and he could only respect that.

Jean hugged his friend tightly, clasping his hand. "Well, breda, I guess this is goodbye until later. Don't worry though, I'll be back!" China gave him a smile, gripped his hand back and then started off with a wave. Jean understood why he didn't say more than that. He didn't want there to be any finality to their parting.

Jean paid Bigga two hundred American dollars to be taken to the resort town of Ocho Rios. The cash advance fueled him and he kept his foot on the accelerator and glued to the floor the whole way. The drive was three hours long and Jean sat staring angrily out of the passenger's side window. Winsome sat quietly in the back seat, drifting in and out of a troubled sleep since her mind was racked with anger and indignation at the way her mother had turned on Jean.

"Why you tell them I was Haitian?" Jean asked Bigga, radiating fury. "Why you tell them I was Haitian and now why is you helping us get out of Kingston? Why?" His voice was low, almost a growl. He liked Bigga in his own way but now he wanted to choke him like he was Dexter or Marlon or Rodrick in the flesh. Bigga looked at Jean for a second and registered his anger. Jean looked ready to kill him with his bare hands. Bigga was used to people cowering at the very sight of him. Not only because he was the constable but because his associations were notorious. Bigga had a lot of power and he'd built a reputation for brutality that made most men hesitate to meet his eyes. Not Jean. In Bigga's mind, that said a lot about the man.

"My youth, remember the day I introduced you to Dexter?" He spoke softly, keeping his eyes on the road in front of him. Not because he was worried about his driving but as if looking through the windshield made whatever he saw in his minds' eye clearer. "...And I told you about him and his family? Well, he and his father work with me...they have their hands in everything that's crooked on that side of the island. Guns, drugs, murder, extortion, you name it and they do it... I been working for dem for many years. I told dem bout you from before but they never see your face until the day Dexter met you. Then, you go and steal the gal deh from him...they take it as a personal insult that someone they extorting, that they consider under them, to steal something from them. I been doing so much wrong for so long that I can at least do something right for once."

There was much left unsaid. Jean shook his head, powerless then, to have done anything to stop the first domino in the chain from falling. He wasn't even mad at Bigga anymore. Bigga was a victim of his own greed and stupidity and there was nothing Jean becoming angry could do to change that. The older man was ashamed of himself and, for a moment, seemed contrite. Then, he sat up and gave Jean a half-hearted smile. "But if they catch me... or see me with you...I'll have to kill you. So, don't make me spot you!" Bigga said in a dead serious tone.

They arrived in town about an hour later. Jean and Winsome said their good bye's to the constable and were on their way. Jean watched the break lights of Bigga's jeep get farther and farther away then he told Winsome that they needed to leave Ocho Rios, because he didn't trust Bigga. She suggested that they go to her family's house in the country where they'd be safer there.

It was late in the evening when they arrived in Ocho Rios but there were still plenty of taxis to be found in the tourist haven. They flagged down a cab within five minutes of Bigga leaving.

"We need to go into the country down in Saint Ann near Moneague, please." Winsome said, very businesslike to the driver.

"Take the back road!" Jean added. He gave the driver $50 American dollars and almost at the speed of sound, the driver turned around and stepped on the gas. He was more than pleased with the money Jean had given him, even for such a long trip. He even followed Winsome's directions without complaint until they arrived at their destination then bid them farewell, making his way back to his home as he had made more than enough money for the night.

The house was a small one, provincial and neat, set far back from the street. As they approached it, Jean gripped the duffel bag in his hand tighter in apprehension. He didn't know if the people behind these doors were friends or foes. He didn't know how much he could trust Winsome's people after the scene her mother made. He didn't know if he would receive that same kind of reception here.

Winsome rapped on the door in hard, short beats.

"Who is it?" the reply came a moment later.

"Ah me, Winsome." She said softly.

There was a murmur of confusion and then the door opened. The young man who stood there stared at them quizzically for a moment then a smile traveled over his features. He was puzzled as to what Winsome was doing there so late at night and who was with her but he obviously loved her very much as there was warmth in his smile.

"Winnie! Whah a gwaan, and why you come here at this time of the night?"

Winsome threw her arms around him in a hug that he reciprocated and he led them into the house. He shook hands with Jean, not taking his eyes off him as Winnie told him what happened. He shook his head and whistled. He'd heard of the Vassels. He'd never had any dealings with them and in his mind that was a good thing. The Vassels were ruthless, corrupt and violent. He shook his head in pity for the two young people standing before him then offered them the small couch in the family's parlor.

He gave them bed linens and some advice about lay low and putting space between themselves and the Vassels then, deep in thought, he retired to his own room for the night.

Jean and Winsome stretched out in relief on the small sofa, hugging each other and breathing deeply for the first time that day. So much had happened in one day. Jean was mentally exhausted but he couldn't rest. The first order of business between them was that of Winsome being pregnant.

"Baby love, why you nah tell me you was going to have a child for me? Why I have to find out like that? You know you can tell me anything," he said kissing her. "We don't hide things from one another."

She massaged his neck and shoulders. "No, mi nah go hide it from you. I wasn't completely sure until last week. I was looking for the right instance to tell you and I was gonna say something when Chinaman left your house but that's when the constable came to the door and here we are. I said it to momma like that because me nah want her fi disrespect the man I love and her grandchild like that!"

Jean had something on his mind for the past few weeks but he'd put it off, unsure of himself. Until that night, when Winsome chose him over her mother and then left all that she'd ever known to be at his side. He was convinced more than ever that she was the woman he wanted to be with for the rest of his life.

He loosened himself from her grip, sat next to her and looked her squarely in the eyes, then asked," Winsome, will you marry me?"

She threw her arms around his neck. "Of course! Of course! Of course I'll marry you. There's no one but you for me to marry!" They hugged each other tightly and when they came back apart, Jean rubbed Winsome's belly, wondering if his child within was a boy or a girl. They kissed and held each other until Winsome drifted to sleep.

Jean, however, was too restless to doze off. He was going through a wide range of emotions including everything from happiness at the prospect of being a father as well as being paranoid that someone had followed them. He decided to stay awake and stand guard with one hand on Winsome's belly, the other gripping his semi automatic forty-five that was tucked in his waist band.

The next day, Patrick and his wife Sonja emerged early from their bedroom. They woke their two young sons, Little Patrick and Steven to start getting ready for school while they got ready to do their morning chores around the house. When Steven and Patrick saw Winsome, they went wild. She was one of their relatives from the city and was so pretty! Often she brought them small gifts. This time she had nothing but her kisses and a fiancée with her. They warmed up to Jean instantly. Kids have a way of knowing good people from bad and. Upon setting eyes on Jean-Paul, they knew he was good. They played with him roughly and he obliged them until Patrick's wife called everyone to the table for a breakfast of salt fish, akee and dumplings. The boys could barely contain their excitement long enough to eat but Jean and Winsome were ravenous.

They ate the whole first serving without pause and, after the two young boys had left for school, embarked on seconds. Afterwards, everyone sat at the table and talked like adults. Jean and Winsome told them the whole story again from the beginning, careful not to omit anything. After everyone finished talking and Winsome revealed that she was pregnant, it was agreed that the best thing for them to do was to go to Haiti and lay low for a little while. Jean wanted to introduce his future bride to his parents and they thought it best for them to be surrounded by love and family as much as possible.

They figured, in a year or so, they could return to Jamaica. Possibly take up residence in the house Winnie's mother owned in the country near Patrick or in another town. It was painfully clear though, that living in Kingston was out of the question for the next few years.

A short while later, Patrick, Jean and Winsome got a ride into Ocho Rios with a man named Popeye. Popeye was a friend of Patrick's who owned an old van. Whenever he was available and Patrick needed to get into town, Popeye would take him with a small fee for gas. Popeye was an easy going old man who'd gotten the nick name thirty years earlier. While fitting a horse for a shoe, the horse started to buck and ended up kicking him in the face with its hind legs. When the smoke cleared, his left eye was taken out and replaced with a glass one. He used to take the glass eye out and scare Patrick and his friends when they were children.

Popeye agreed to run Patrick and the others in to Ocho Rios where Patrick was to meet his associate, Thomas. Thomas had a cigarette boat that he used to give tourists rides. This was his front for his smuggling operation, which was his main bread and butter. Patrick knew that for the right price his friend Thomas would smuggle anything out of the country and maybe even as far as the southern tip of the US, in Florida.

It was an hour's drive to the dock in Ocho Rios from where they were in the country. When they reached, Patrick had them all wait in the van while he went to look for Thomas in the area of the docks where he usually was. It was better for him to go alone, he reasoned, in case Dexter or his father had goons looking for them in Ocho Rios.

It took a short while for Patrick to find Thomas. After the two men went through the usual greetings and inquiries about their health, Patrick wasted no time getting to the point. The longer Jean and Winsome remained in Jamaica, the more of a chance for the Vassels to catch up with them and the more danger they were all in. Patrick told him that his cousin and her fiancé needed a speedy getaway to Haiti. It was an unusual request. Most people didn't leave one poor Caribbean country for another. However, Thomas saw a good chance to make money off the desperation of others so he replied, "yeah, mon, no problem. I can run them to Haiti for you but I had a tour today... and its still day light. I'll cancel my tour for you today because it's urgent that they leave today, but for me canceling the tour its going to cost them forty thousand dollars! If you all can come up with that kind of money right away, then we have a deal..."

Patrick balled up his face, angrily asking, "Why so much mon, that's a lot of money! I don't know if they can come up with that kind of money!"

Thomas wasn't concerned. He knew they would pay whatever he wanted. "Because I had a group of Americans that were going to pay me $500 American dollars and you know when the Americans have a good trip, they leave a nice tip too. So, I figure to miss out on the American money, I might as well get paid double to also cover the tips I'm going to miss, seen?"

It was a rip off and Patrick knew it. No Americans would pay him $500 to tour the coast in a rinky- dink boat. There were tours which operated glass bottomed boats that charged less than a fraction of that but it was urgent for the two of them to leave and the boatman knew they'd pay him whatever he wanted. With his face still frowned into an angry ball, Patrick returned to the van with what he thought was very bad news for Jean and Winsome.

To his surprise, Jean agreed to pay it. Patrick didn't feel it was worth it. Thomas was charging what anyone else would have asked to make a trip to Florida. To go to a little poor island that everyone was trying to leave, not go to. But, the value of his woman and unborn child's safety was paramount to Jean and he needed peace of mind during Winsome's pregnancy.

They bid farewell to Popeye and made their way with Patrick to where the scoundrel awaited. Without any fanfare, Jean paid Thomas half the money up front and told him he'd get the rest when they arrived in Haiti.

"Never pay full price till you get where you are going!" Jean said in a playful tone. Yet, his manner was dead serious and it occurred to Thomas that the deadliest man was a desperate man. He nodded in agreement to Jean's statement and went to do a systems check. He was about to receive one thousand American dollars, for one day's work, and that was a small fortune. He wouldn't jeopardize that for the sake of any petty arguments.

A few moments later, Thomas was done with the systems check and they were all set to go.

"Take care of my cousin, hear?" Patrick said before he broke his grip on Jean's hand. Jean gave him a slight nod and a smile. He was thankful for all the man had done for them since their arrival and he considered him a friend. Patrick hugged Winsome tightly and kissed her, trying to infuse her with strength from his positive energy. He felt bad for her and the situation the two of them found themselves in and he wished more than anything that he could have told them to stay with him but he had his own family, his wife and his children to think of. He kissed Winsome on the forehead and helped her into the boat.

Their ride got a tad bumpy once the boat reached top speed in the open sea. However, the sheer beauty of the ocean itself was calming. They relaxed under the sultry blue sky and the sun's loving rays, determined to make the best of whatever they faced. To Winsome's delight, a school of dolphins swam alongside the boat for some time, jumping in and out of the water, close enough that she could touch them. The tranquility of the voyage made Jean certain that everything would be alright.

CHAPTER SEVEN

They arrived in Haiti, a little over six hours after they'd left. Jean knew of a remote dock by Port Au Prince, where he'd grown up. He and Thomas guided the boat there with ease. The sailing inland was smooth and, with very little correction, an experienced navigator could slide right in. Haiti had no coast guard or navy or border patrol. The water's edge was inhabited not by the rich, as in all the rest of the world, but by those who had packed up and moved there. Some places along the coast were crowded with earthen abodes. These were little more than four walls and planks laid lengthwise for a roof, designed to welcome in the breeze and provide someplace to sleep at night after easy days on the beach. Other places hosted lavish mansions and compounds. Some areas though, especially those that were bordered by large rocks, were deserted and served as harbors.

It took some time to find the particular dock Jean had in mind but they did and, when Jean stepped ashore, he felt that things had come full circle. He was back in the land of his birth, with his pregnant woman at his side and an uncertain future before him. Carrying the duffel bag over his shoulder, he paid Thomas the rest of his money and watched the boat slide away into the night.

Holding hands, they made their way down the raggedy old dock onto a sandy dirt trail. The small path was snaky and confusing to strangers but allowed the natives who knew it to cut through the bush in less than a third of the time. They walked leisurely, Winsome noticing the small things like the trees and the way the rocks and small piece of glassine debris shone like gems. It was a truly beautiful island, lush with life and sound. The walk was fascinating to Winsome and every so often Jean stopped to show her a landmark or to tell her some funny story that happened under this or that tree. They arrived in Lacaye two hours after leaving the dock at Port Au Prince, holding hands and laughing.

Jean felt good to be home. He didn't stop to salute anyone on his way, knowing that on the small island, news traveled fast. By the morning everyone and their mother would literally know that he had returned home, with a woman. There was no possibility of keeping that a secret. He wanted to rest rather than entertain everyone with stories of his travels and adventures, as would be expected of him. A homecoming from anywhere, even from different parts of the island, was always a big deal. He knew that there would be scores of people coming to visit the next day. He avoided the main paths on his way home, luckily missing the most talkative and inquisitive neighbors.

Jean was excited at the prospect of introducing his parents to Winsome and vice versa but, as soon as he saw the house, his excitement faded and something like panic settled in.

In Haiti, at that time, there was no electricity. Most houses didn't have bathrooms indoors and because of the tropical climate and sometimes intense heat, life was lived primarily outdoors and in the community. Neighbors were plenty and there was always a group around, talking and laughing as they did their endless chores. The women maintained their neighborhoods as one big family. All of the mothers you knew growing up had as much jurisdiction over you as your own mother. Even at 30 years old with a wife and family, you would not be considered a gran moun (or full grown adult) while you were still expected to show the utmost respect to those older than you. To play your part in the community. Meals were collective. Eating selfishly was something only the habitans, who were considered savages and strange, did. Every night, neighbors brought each other food and visited as the sun went down. That was why Jean filled with fear at the sight of a darkened, abandoned house.

In his entire life, he had never seen any signs of life at his home and he quickened his pace to investigate. He walked into the house from their small porch, into the salon or living room. There was a lamp hanging in the doorway of the salles a manger (dining room) and he took it down and lit it with a long match from the corner where they kept them. Then, he walked through the house. The house was humble, four small rooms and a kitchen on the back porch. As they did not have family abroad, to send them money to buy store-bought things, all of the furniture had been crafted by people who lived close by and there were no decorations or eye candy frills that served no purpose. Everything in the home was necessary and utilitarian but well kept and beautifully made. His mother had been a meticulous housekeeper and, as Jean-Paul wiped his hands across their things and came up with dust, he knew something was wrong.

He went back outside, this time looking for a familiar face. There was no one. He looked in the direction of the two closest homes, the small dwellings of two women who had practically raised him since birth and whose children he had spent every minute of his young life in the company of but there was absolute stillness, nothing.

Winsome stood behind him, watching him, knowing that something was wrong. "Baby… is there something wrong?" she asked, already knowing the answer. His face was hard and he didn't look at her.

"Let's just get some rest for right now and we'll be able to find out everything in the morning," he said.

CHAPTER EIGHT

They slept in his parent's room, something that felt strange and wrong. It intensified Jean-Paul's feeling that something horrible had happened. His mother was the only woman in Haiti with only one child, it seemed. All of the other families he knew were lavish and boasted ten or twelve or six or seven robust youngsters. Even in the poorest families, children were considered God's greatest gift and the families who lived closest to him. Man Elliette and Matante Marie Lourdes, both had housefuls of human blessings. Man Elliette had eleven living children and Matante Marie Lourdes had fourteen. There was no way that they would have all gone out of the same night or that none of the children had come out to see who was going into his parents place when he'd arrived.

He tossed and turned all night, his body fatigued by the travel and the excitement of all that had happened in only two days but his mind was restless and anxious.

When he woke the next morning, the sun sat in his window where the crescent moon had been the night before. He almost forgot where he was for an instant. When he felt Winsome's arm, the warmth of her flesh jolted him. He only took a second to regain his bearings then he tickled the bottoms of her feet until she twisted and stretched out of her slumber.

"It's morning already? It feels like I just laid down," she grumbled. He kissed her with messed up hair, morning breath and all, then slid out of the bed and made his way to their salles de bain (bath room). There were no western style bathrooms in Haiti at that time. Most people still used outhouses, dark little hovels with nothing but a box over a deep hole.

The box had a circle cut out in the top of it and, as a child, it had been Jean-Paul's scariest nightmare that he would fall into that hole. For bathing, lucky people had pipes or tuyos that piped water in. The water wasn't clean enough to drink and it was room temperature as the pipes were often unheated but they got the job done. They bathed in huge metal or porcelain stand alone tubs and it wasn't uncommon to see a simple shower rigged in a semi private spot. These showers were usually just a pipe fastened overhead somehow, with the water trained to run into rivulets that fed a garden or into a larger pool that fed the well. The unlucky had to get water from communal pumps, some times quite a distance away. They assigned these unsavory jobs to the family's children.

Though the people weren't formally educated, there was an understanding. That while rich, white nations had technology, they had technique and always found ingenious ways to deal with the lack of material goods. There was no sense of competition with regards to materialism. You had or you didn't have but if you needed, your neighbors who after a point became kin, were more than happy to give, knowing that someday you would do the same for them.

He showed Winsome the outhouse, which she found absolutely horrifying and then the area where they cooked and their living room. He showed her the communal well. Growing up, it had been a landmark, a meeting place and base for games of chase. It was shared by all of the families of the area, despite its close proximity to his home and, as a child, he'd fetched from that well millions of times. This time, because of the strange things that he'd noted since his return, he checked the well for debris or carcasses. Maybe, whoever had done whatever had happened to his family and neighbors had poisoned their well also. He couldn't take any chances.

Not seeing any signs of foul play, Jean tied the pail he'd bought unto the corded rope then lowered it into the well. He brought it back up a minute later, filled. He then detached the pail and carried the water over to a large enamel tub, bigger than a cauldron. A full grown adult could sit in there and often that's how it was used. In this instance, he was filling it with water to boil for drinking.

Jean made the trip thrice more and then Winsome, tired of standing there like a decoration, began to help him. In four trips working together, they had the cauldron filled. Jean then went through the process of lighting the fire under it, using a wood called bwois pain. It took time but eventually the small flame caught.

While he worked, Winsome caught her breath and really took a look at the small house. It was a modest home that consisted of the dining area where everyone would eat. The living room where the family would congregate. Also a back room that was sectioned off into two rooms for Jean's parents and his quarters. After she saw her new living accommodations, which had no electricity or running water in the house and was in stark contrast to what she had been accustomed to in Jamaica. She noted that something had seemingly gone wrong with Jean's parents. The totality and the gravity of their situation slowly began to sink in. Therefore, Winsome realized the seriousness of their plight for the first time, at that moment.

For all the wailing of the whites and humanitarian aid workers commenting on Haiti. Most Haitians (who weren't political dissidents) lived what they considered a good life. Fortune wasn't measured by what car, if any one had one, or what clothes you wore. Again, family was first and foremost. Having intelligent sons and daughters you could send to school, who could emigrate abroad and make a better life for the whole family was the ultimate prize for every Haitian mother. The money these children sent back was enough to take care of not only their nuclear family but all the assorted cousins, uncles, aunts and relations who made up Haitian life.

Kinship wasn't necessarily dictated by blood but through experience. The women, whose children you had played with since birth. Who made clothes for your sister and who often sent you to run little errands, was without question an aunt. The children you'd gone to school with all your life, who were your constant companions, whose home you often ate at. The one's whose hand me downs you might have worn and vice versa, they were of course your cousins. The old men who watched disapprovingly as you ran when you should have walked. The one's who carved little flutes for all the neighborhood children and who helped your father when he wanted to add on to the house were naturally your uncles. Even at thirty, forty or fifty, these relationships were to be honored.

He surveyed the empty houses again, feeling the acute strangeness of not seeing Man Elliete, Matante Marie Lourdes or their many children. Jean felt the same pressure and responsibility to finding out what had become of those families then, as he did to finding his own parents. Without wasting another moment, he and Winsome left the house and made their way to Port Au Prince to find Pierre.

Winsome was soaking up her surroundings, studying the faces and the merchandise they offered. It was a strange, different place but familiar nonetheless. There was nothing here that explained to her the hatred her mother had shown or the disdain she'd often heard in the voices of some people when speaking of Haitians.

They looked like regular people to her, all shades, sizes and heights. She couldn't understand their words but their expressions and gestures were the same as any one else she'd seen. Winsome found herself trying to follow conversations and guessing at transactions to pass the time. She was enjoying the exercise, holding tightly to Jean's muscular arm as they walked. Then she noticed a rickety old jeep slow down as it passed them. The jeep pulled over and seemed to be waiting for them. Winsome felt a flash of nervousness. The military feel of the vehicle made her edgy and she began to wonder if the Vassels hadn't sent someone to the island to find them. She remembered Thomas' ugly greedy face and wondered if he hadn't told someone as soon as he'd returned about his last minute passengers to Haiti.

As they got closer, the driver of the jeep, a high yellow man with red hair and freckles, got out and began making his way towards them. Winsome began reciting the Lord's Prayer, her eyes not leaving his face, trying to send Jean small messages by tugging at his arm. Winsome was reciting the prayer frantically under her breath, studying his yellow, scowling face. Her whole life flashed before her eyes, from the time she was a toddler playing with her mother, to the times she was jealous of her older sister Gwen, to her asshole ex-lover Dexter, to the day Jean had laid him flat on his back playing football, then to Jean and how much she loved him in addition to all the wonderful times they'd had together and the many times they'd made sweet beautiful love.

She pulled down on Jean's arm again, trying to get him to focus on what she was seeing. He was in his own world. Before she could call out, he began pulling her faster, in the direction of the stranger. When they came to be about five feet from each other, the two of them broke into wide grins and clasped hands. At the same time, they began speaking rapidly in their patois.

They were ecstatic about being reunited. That much was obvious. She gave him a small smile as they talked, hearing her name every so often.

"Ces't Winsome," Jean said, in creole, pointing to Winsome. Then, he spoke to her. "This is my friend Pierre, my best friend in Haiti, the one I was looking for."

They shook hands, exchanging pleasant smiles. "Allo, ki jon ou ye?" Or hello, how are you?" Pierre asked.

The words were foreign but Winsome smiled back to let him know that she was fine, reasonably certain that he'd inquired about her health. He nodded and went back to talking to Jean.

They were engrossed in their conversation for the better part of an hour, while Winsome stood in the shade, watching people go by. She was tired of standing and bored from waiting, but she knew Jean had many questions and she wouldn't interrupt.

CHAPTER NINE

In Jamaica, Donavan Vassel radiated fury as he walked through the halls of the hospital where his son was being treated. His stride was more than angry, it was violently heated and every single person he passed felt the energy flaming around him. No one met his eye. Everyone conveniently remembered patients that needed tending to and dipped into the rooms or pretended they were needed there, any where, but the direction he was walking in.

His son lay in a hospital bed with tubes attached to him, feeding him and breathing for him. There was a possibility that he might have lasting brain damage if he recuperated, the petrified Indian doctor had whispered. Donavan nearly throttled the man. He wanted to make someone pay and, for that instant, anyone would do. When he calmed down a bit, he refocused on the true object of his rage and vengeance. The stinking Haitian who'd beaten his son. He would make him pay for this!

It wasn't just the beating. When Dexter fell, he'd struck the base of his head. Jean had fought him fair and square and hadn't hurt him anymore than Dexter would have gladly hurt him if he'd won the fight instead. Dexter's condition was as much due to fate as to the other man's martial skills but, in his blind fury, Donavan would never accept that notion.

The next day after Donavan visited Dexter in the hospital, he lay anxiously in wait to see Bigga. It had been almost a whole 24 hours since he'd sent Bigga to find Jean Paul and whoever was with him. Especially that slut of a bitch Winsome and that God damned Chinaman, he thought to himself. Finally, at about three that afternoon, Percy, with Bigga behind him, walked into the den where Donavan awaited.

"Fuck a gwaan? Where are they? You find dem? I thought I told you to let me kill them when you found them?" Donavan said without preamble. He wanted to get to business as soon as he saw the two of them. This matter was urgent and he wouldn't allow anyone or anything to trivialize it.

"No don," Bigga started cautiously. "Mi look everywhere in town and me nah see a one of dem."

Donavan breathed out hard, annoyed. "Go get me all dem boys in the back who was wit mi Dexter yesterday. Matter fact, blindfold them and put dem in the van outside."

Percy and Bigga rounded up all six of the young men who were with Dexter the day before, at the soccer game. They blindfolded them and packed them into two non-descript white vans. Two of the six men were Rodrick, Donavan's nephew through Dwayne and Marlon, who was Pudgy's son. Donavan hopped into the van a minute later and ordered Percy to drive to an area known as "Back o' wall."

Percy obeyed and put the van in reverse, then began making his way over to his said destination. He felt sad though because, he knew Donavan was going to more than likely murder his own nephew and Pudgy's son as well.

About half an hour later, Percy reached their destination. Before them lay the large gully the government used as a sanitation dump but was also used by Donavan's crew to dispose of bodies! Donavan lined all six boys up side by side on their knees and, in a cold blooded, voice began giving them a lecture.

"Take care of mi Dexter and make sure you save him from himself is all I ask you. No. Me pay you to do and you can't even get that right. So, what you take I fi joke? Well, guess who the joke is on now?"

With that, a deafening round of gunfire went off. Donavan started from left to right, giving his victims each two shots . One to the back of the head and another to the neck execution style causing a pinkish mist to fill the air from the wholes that were bore into their heads as puddles of plasma and grey brain matter oozed out of what remained of their skulls. The blind folded heads of the young men were nearly knocked completely off from the thunderous impact of his giant forty five.

"Wait!" Bigga pleaded. "Wait, please don't kill your nephew and mi likkle cousin dem. Please! They are our family!" Bigga said with a passion and an urgency that caused Donavan to pause and snap out of the murderous rage and trance that he'd lapsed into.

Donavan took a glance at what he had done and it gave him pause. He was still angry but he'd snapped out of his killing trance.

"What did you say? How you mean family? If they was so much family, they would have been protecting their cousin yesterday, wouldn't they? Wouldn't they?" The rage swelled up inside him again and he started to aim. The two young boys began pleading for their lives.

"Please Uncle Donavan. We're sorry and it won't happen again! Please...just let the two a we live...please!"

He surveyed them coldly at first but then with great joy, Bigga wiped beads of sweat from his brow when he saw Donavan ease up and put the gun in his waist band. Donavan waved his hand, signaling to Percy and Bigga to let Rodrick and Marlon off their knees and to remove their blindfolds. When they both were on their feet and had finished wiping the tears from their eyes, Bigga noticed that they'd both pissed their pants.

"Come here, the two of you and listen me!" Donavan ordered the two nineteen year olds. "I know this Haitian guy is...dangerous. But, know this, if I ever give you something this important again and you nah get it right, you go end up like your bredren in the ditch, seen? Don't worry about being scared of nobody else, be scared of what I'll do fi unoo if you let something go wrong again. Fear me, more than you fear the wrath of God!" He emphatically stated then suddenly gave them both a smack to their faces wit his gun still in hand.

Donavan's tone was flat and his eyes hooded like a King Cobra. His nephew by blood and Pudgy's, son who he'd raised like a nephew, both nodded, understanding just how close they'd come to death. As they both held their faces withering in pain from being slightly pistol whipped.

Bigga got in the back of the van with Rodrick and Marlon while Percy drove. Donavan was in the passenger seat beside Bigga still radiating enough searing white hatred to make everyone in the van sweat. Bigga's heart danced on the back of his tongue as they drove through the streets. He was praying to his God that no one had spotted him with Jean and Winsome the night before. Donavan had killed those boys easily, boys that he'd known from a pickney. Boys whose mothers he would see everyday, whose family trees he knew from their roots. He'd killed them easily and was ready to do the same to his own flesh and blood, to his own nephews. In Bigga's mind, that more than anything told him all he needed to know about what Donavan Vassel would easily do to him. He was nothing like his son because his up bringing and rise to the status of a Don was totally different from Dexter's.

Jamaica, 1935

Donavan Fitzroy Vassell had been raised by his young mother and her family in the ghetto of Kingston's Tiverly Gardens. Where he'd grown up wasn't prosperous and, by the age of thirteen, he was a full fledged bandit in pursuit of the kind of wealth that the British colonialists flaunted. He caused his family nothing but grief with his shananigins. From robbing people on the streets to terrorizing the other boys, the visits from the constable and magistrates were constant. He was like a pariah. The families he'd grown up around were poor but proud people, who had high standards and ambition for their children. They didn't want their kids associating with the likes of Donavan Vassel and, after a time, some of the adults even began to fear him.

By the age of 15, his mother and the local magistrate had enough of his wild ways. He was sentenced to two years hard labor in a prison at the foot hills of Jamaica's famous Blue Mountains.

Four months into his sentence, almost doubled over from the racking pain that tortured his back so he escaped into the darkness of the night. He ran for dear life, forcing himself to walk upright and move swiftly. He had worked the mines without ceasing and he'd come to understand why mining was considered "back –breaking" labor. His muscles ached and he felt like the bones in his back were painfully out of alignment. The night he escaped, by the light of the moon like a slave, he would have preferred to die than to ever go back. He wandered the deep bush of Jamaica's interior for four days, with no food and water. He didn't care as long as he was free from what he considered slavery and torture as man was not meant to be put in a cage. He kept moving, like a madman, farther and farther away from that hell until his legs gave out beneath him and he collapsed under a tree.

When he awoke, there was a group of Maroons standing over him, engrossed in a debate about what they should do with him. He was too weak to speak on his own behalf and that was enough to sway even the most cautious heart so they took him amongst them and nursed him back to health.

He lived there for a season, learning their customs and culture. It was the most peaceful period of his life and, during that time, he thought he would leave a changed man. It was also the time he learned everything he could possibly have wanted to know about ganja including how to cultivate and harvest it. The Maroons used it in their daily rituals, seeking spiritual awareness and such but Donavan made the two day trek back to Kingston, after he'd left their camp with nothing but a small pack of food, and used that knowledge to build an empire. The entire experience, even the time he'd spent in the mining camp, became priceless to Donavan as an adult.

The ganja he'd stashed away while he was amongst the Maroons became the first ganja he sold on streets of Kingston. His clientele were tourists and sailors in the British Navy, who were blown away by the strength and flavor of the pure grown herb he possessed. He used the seeds to plant a new crop in a secret spot outside of Kingston but, while he waited for that to grow, he'd make his way back along the paths into the interior to grab some more ganja. This went well and, for a moment, things settled into a pleasant rhythm.

Then, someone started stealing from his crop. It was an older man about twenty-five, dark-skinned and about five foot eight. Donavan saw the perpetrator a day after he discovered his crops had been tampered with. He'd patiently been waiting to see who was stealing from him ....the master thief. He'd hide out of sight in a group of palm trees a few yards away from his crop and couldn't believe what he was seeing. The dark-skinned man had a cloth sack and was freely taking his stash.

"Hey you deh! Stop what you're doing that ganja belongs to me" Donavan said excitedly as he slowly made his way toward the man responsible for giving him grief.

"What? Your name isn't any where on these here plants mon! Besides the Earth is meant to be harvested and shared, and no one but the almighty own the Earth my lad!" The stranger told Donavan not at all taking him seriously. At first, by the urgency of Donavan's voice, the stranger expected to see some one he deemed his equal in age. Not some scrawny light skinned curly headed kid.

"Tis no laughing matter mon! I'm serious put down the bag and leave and you'll live," Donavan said in a dead serious tone. By then, Donavan had walked with in arm's reach of the stranger. Still not taking him serious, the man just reached out and smacked him in the face. The force of the blow turned Donavan in the opposite direction and caused him to fall to the ground.

The man stood over Donavan and let out a sadistic laugh. "My lad you must learn how to respect your elders!" the stranger said while still holding the sack in his left hand and offering to help Donavan up with his right. Striking him proved to be a mistake on the behalf of the stranger. Donavan began to get up. He grabbed the stranger's right hand with his left hand. Once Donavan got to his feet, he swiftly brandished a pocket knife and repeatedly plunged it into the man's torso. The last time he plunged the knife into the stranger's body, he stuck it in the center of his chest twisting it hoping to hit the man's heart to open the wound wider.

Even if Donavan hadn't punctured his victim's lungs or heart, it was almost certain the man was a goner. The blade Donavan used had been dipped in garlic. By dipping the blade in garlic, it made the wound sting even worse and almost impossible for it to be stitched because the garlic ate away at the wound and made the skin very thin. This was a very ancient technique that dated back to Africa, used when rival tribes would go to war. Donavan had learned this deadly and malicious tactic from the Maroons who retained much of their ancestry and history from Africa.

Indeed, it was a mistake on the part of the older stranger. Now with him lying on his back attempting to get up, he knew it was a fatal one. The man stood on his hands and knees desperately gasping for air and trying to summon the strength to get up. However, it was too late he was severely wounded. Donavan's knife had managed to pierce his lungs and they were filling up with his own blood. Sadly for the stranger, the more he squirmed about on his hands and knees, the faster he lost blood from his other wounds. Then, finally, the stranger collapsed to the ground and stood still forever more. In the end, his lungs filled up with plasma and he drowned in his own blood.

This wasn't a pretty sight for the faint at heart however, for Donavan, this was his coming of age. He reasoned that if he could survive hard labor, escape and survive in the jungle then he was totally complete as a man because he knew he had the heart to kill. Some could kill if you made them angry or maybe they had to defend their family's honor. But, this was totally different. This was personal. He didn't simply shoot his victim from a distance. He'd used a knife up close and personal. He felt the life of the man leaving from his body with every blow. Donavan liked the feeling of having killed another human being and knew for sure that he now could do it again at his leisure.

Donavan stood there for a moment and stared at the man's lifeless body then contemplated his next move. Nonchalantly, Donavan wiped the blood of his foe off his knife onto the shirt of the dead man. Then, he dragged the body about ten yards to some near by shrubs to provide cover for the man's corpse. Once the body was secure and out of sight, he made his way back towards town in the area where he moved his ganja. For about four hours, he sold his ganja as if nothing at all had happened.

Once he finished hawking his goods for the day, he paid a visit to one of his old associates, from his thieving days, named Pudgy. Pudgy was a sixteen years old dark-skinned boy with an appetite that could feed a small country. He and Pudgy were somewhat polar opposites. Donavan stole for survival, while Pudgy was from a more stable middle class back ground who stole for a thrill and extra treats to fill his enormous gut.

At sixteen, Pudgy stood about five foot six and weighed about two hundred and twenty five pounds. Most of the weight was concentrated in his mid-section. Donavan went by Pudgy to ask if he could borrow a machete. Pudgy agreed and also gave him a brown cloth potato sack to carry the machete in. This gave Donavan an idea. He went around town searching for more potato sacks. He found himself rummaging through the garbage cans in the back of a local restaurant and managed to find two more large potato sacks. When he'd found his supplies, it was time to activate his plan.

Donavan made his way back to his victim's corpse. With only about three and a half hours of sun light left, he had to work fast. With all his might Donavan began swinging the machete at the back of the man's neck. In just two mighty swings of the blade the man's head was detached from the rest of his body. Donavan held back from gagging, not so much as from seeing the veins and tendons of the mans neck, but from the ghastly smell releasing from the decomposing body he'd opened up under the humid eighty-five degree Caribbean sun.

Donavan periodically held his breath as he swung the blade with precision at the ends of the man's limbs. After awhile, he'd gotten used to the smell and stopped holding his breath all together. Then after about an hour and a half, he'd finally finished separating the man's limbs so they would fit in the potato sacks he'd brought with him. Afterwards, Donavan made his way back to Kingston and got himself a room and a meal at a local flop house in his old stomping grounds of Tiverly Gardens.

The following morning, Donavan stole some bed sheets from out of one of his neighbor's rooms in the flop house. Then, he wrapped the blade in the sheets so he could return it to Pudgy. And, once he gave the blood stained machete to him, Pudgy had a fit.

"Jesus Christ, Donavan. Me momma a go kill me when she see all the blood on this here blade! What happened... you chop someone to death with this here thing, boss?" Pudgy said jokingly as he playfully jabbed Donavan in the shoulder. He noticed Donavan wasn't laughing and had a sinister smirk on his face.

"Gwan easy now mon, the blood is no big deal. You can clean it off with vinegar and alcohol, seen. You want to make some money my youth?" Donavan probed in a flat yet trusting tone.

"Yeah Mon! Shot back Pudgy quickly and nervously.

"See it ya! I need you to help me burry my dead dog. He got too old and I had to put him to sleep. What say you? Will you help me dig a deep enough hole for five pounds?"

Five pounds was more than enough for Pudgy to get his hands dirty. At the time, in 1946, the island was still under British colonial rule and five pounds could go a long way for Pudgy,

"Hush now mon, you wasting time talking about it while we could be getting it done," Pudgy hastily said.

Donavan knew he could count on his old partner in crime....if he dangled a small reward in front of his face. Pudgy put on his shoes and told his little brother to tell their mother that he went to work as a day laborer digging ditches with a friend. Just like that, the former partners in crime were on their way to Donavan's secret location.

They got there by foot about an hour later. Pudgy began complaining about the hot morning sun, and Donavan wanted to hurry up so he could get back to town. Finally, they started digging with two small shovels Pudgy's mother used when she worked from time to time at a local sugar cane plantation.

It took them about three hours but they managed to dig about a two foot wide four foot deep hole. Donavan took a breather and began playing the boss role by ordering Pudgy to take the sacks from where he had them and throw them into the hole they'd dug.

Once Pudgy began to tug at the potato sacks, he knew by the weight of the sacks that it wasn't a dead dog. He went along with the program with out saying a word. After all a deal was a deal and all Pudgy was concerned with was his five pounds.

An hour passed and they were finished filling the hole with dirt. As promised, Donavan reached in his back pocket of his dungarees and handed Pudgy a five pound note from a wad of bills he was carrying. Pudgy took note of the size of Donavan's bill fold and told him when ever he needed him for any more jobs not to hesitate in letting him know. A warm current shot up the base of Donavan's spine, past his neck and ears then on to his cheeks, causing him to smile at hearing those words. He shook his head in agreement then shot back...

"Yeah mon I have plenty of work lined up for the two a we seen."

As they walked back toward town, Donavan gave Pudgy a nice sized bud of ganja in addition to his other pay. Pudgy just smiled examined the bud then put it into his front pocket. The two juvenile crime prodigies finally made their way back to Pudgy's where they put back the shovels where they belonged and parted company for the day.

Immediately after Donavan left Pudgy, he made his way back to the flop house where he was staying. He washed up then went to bed without as much as a flinch and didn't even dare think of having a bad dream. Donavan always knew he had the heart to kill, however the reason nor the opportunity never presented itself until he found the stranger pouching on his secret crop.

With Donavan having, in cold blood, murdered another man, who as far as he could tell at least ten years his senior, he'd conquered his last fear and inhibition which was doubt and remorse. Deep down, Donavan always knew he would have to kill someone, but he also feared that he might be haunted by the experience. He feared that, in his heart of hearts, his conscience would eat him alive. However, it was quite the opposite.

His reaction of his first murder was a business move and nothing personal. Besides, he warned the man several times to leave but he took him for a joke. Even though Donavan was generally easy going he knew the satisfaction of getting rid of a foe and nipping a problem in the bud as soon as he spotted it. True this was his first homicide, however the rush of adrenaline and power he felt, when he actually killed the stranger, was like nothing he ever experienced before.

He was intoxicated with a feeling of apathy and narcissism, completely absorbed in the moment - so much so that he, in fact, felt as if his veins were on fire and a pulsating tingle in his soloplexes. The one problem he was having was he didn't know rather it came from being able to kill or from getting away with murder so smoothly. He wrestled with the idea for a few hours and finally came to the conclusion it was a mixture of both.

It had been about a year since Donavan escaped from the labor camp and made his way back to Kingston. Things were going pretty well for him. As he lay there in the bed, staring at the ceiling fan go around in circles, he thought about his past and thought about where he wanted to go in the future. He'd taken the arrogant stranger's life in cold blood and there was no changing that. So, he was compiling a plan to expand for his immediate future. Thoughts of how easy it was for the stranger to find his crop and start taking as much as he wanted with liberty danced through Donavan's mind.

His grandmother had always counseled him about the wisdom of learning from the mistakes he'd made in life. "Do right the first time and you won't have to do again," his grandmother, Icelene, had often preached. He saw the errors of his ways and he was determined to not let her down. He had to deal with the thief in a way that would teach him as well as any other interlopers that stealing from him was the worst they could do. He wouldn't use the garlic laced cut for this. He needed brute, unmistakable force. He needed a gun.

He also needed an army. He set his mind about the business of finding some brothers trustworthy enough to help him in his war on poverty. He needed soldiers, not captains. The less people at the top of his organization, the less people who knew where the stash was, the less people who had details on the moves he made, the better. Even though Donavan was a criminal, he wasn't a stupid man. Not by a long shot. More than anyone he knew, Donavan studied. He studied how others did things, history and military strategy.

He had watched the men in every part of his life and he'd seen that some were leaders and some were followers and some, the rarest of them all, were Dons. Donavan made it his determined idea that he would become not only a Don, but a legendary Don.

The next morning, on the run in plain sight, he made his way back to Tiverly Gardens. He was technically a fugitive and hadn't been home since he'd been taken off to jail but that didn't worry him. He was anxious to see familiar faces and as disgusted, as they might have been with him a year before, he knew time had a way of healing wounds. He knew Tiverly Gardens was where his best chances of finding what he was looking for lay.

He had a mental list of people he needed to see, and at the top of the list was his old crime partner, Percy. At eighteen years old, Percy was a veteran of every street war. He was absolutely fearless and was the one who'd first got Donavan started robbing and stealing. Percy was a general, a magnetic sort of person who could incite anyone to do anything. Donavan wanted him on his team at all cost.

Pudgy was next. Pudgy was eager and daring, the type who just wanted to see something happen, no matter how violent or destructive. Donavan had taught him everything he knew and brought him up through the ranks like Percy had done him. There was no question of Pudgy's absolute loyalty in Donavan's mind.

He found Percy first, posted up on the back wall of the old tavern called Zanzabar as though he were holding the joint up on his back all by himself. He'd started hanging there doing dirt with an older crowd, once he got tired of small time petty thievery. He stood outside as though he weren't doing much but his sharp eyes didn't miss anything. Donavan didn't doubt for a second that he was somehow making money as he roasted under the infernal heat of the midday sun.

"Percy, whah a gwaan wit you, my youth?" Donavan exclaimed.

Percy focused on him without expression at the sound of his voice, at first thinking he must be imagining the sight of his most trusted friend. He rubbed his eyes and, when Donavan was still there, he called back "A whoo dat, Donavan?"

They were already walking towards each other and when they met, Percy gripped him in a tight embrace, gripping his right hand. "A long time me nah see you! I thought you were doing four years in dat labor camp, what happen to you mon?" He asked while giving him the once-over.

Donavan gave him a big smile, stretched out, really feeling like he was home. "Yeah mon, dem a give me four years but, when they wasn't looking, me run fi mi life! Mi run for four days, all the way back to Kingston! But me low still bredren, in case the constable ah go look for me!"

CHAPTER TEN

Later, as the two friends burned a spliff, Donavan told Percy of his budding ganja empire and how he was trying to expand his operation immediately. He told him of his need to have a crew to help him move his product as well as provide him with muscle to keep other competitors in line. He told Percy he needed him on his side because he knew he could trust him. Percy explained that he was currently employed by Donald who was the local Don. Once he knew Percy was affiliated with Donald, it was even better because nobody would try Donald - not even a little bit. The other boy smiled, double happy to see his long time friend and ecstatic that his friend had come home with a business proposition for him.

They agreed to split the money sixty-forty and, in two days time, they met back up at the Zanzibar. This had been enough time to spread the word. As well as give Donavan time to come up with a nice quantity, double what he was selling on his own. Percy distributed the herb to patrons of the Zanzibar, in small bundles weighing just a little over a gram for one pound. The results were amazing. Eventhough Percy had told only a few people, they told people who in turn told more people and so on and so on.

In fact, the product was moving so fast word was getting out that Percy was selling. He knew that he'd have to cut Donald in or face a stiff penalty. In just two weeks of Percy selling it by grams, they had moved more than a whole pound of ganja. There were others who sold ganja in the area. However, none of them had anything as good as Donavan's Blue Mountain crop. Also no one else was backed by Donald.

To avoid any conflict with Donald, Percy set up the meeting between the three of them. Donald was rarely seen in the area because he kept a low profile. He stayed nearby in case there was something his underlings couldn't handle because he bore in mind the old saying, out of sight, out of mind. However, Donald was from that area and had been doing dirt since he was a babe at his mother's breast. So he was high on the royal police's priority list and only showed his face when it was necessary. Percy assured Donald that it would be well worth his time. Donald then agreed to the meeting.

The next morning Percy came to get Donavan from the flophouse where he was laying low and told him of the meeting he'd set up for later that night. Donavan was ecstatic about meeting Donald. The man's reputation was fearsome. Donald was a bad mon legend and the thought that he was going to meet the great man filled Donavan with anxious anticipation. It felt like an eternity as he waited for the day to go by but, when he entered the Zanzibar Club later that evening something, his gut told him the meeting would be well worth any wait.

There were a lot of women in the club that night, many more than the last time but he paid them no mind. He was there on business and all of his thoughts were arranged around what he'd come to do. Percy was more lighthearted and exchanged pleasantries with everyone around him as they drank at the bar.

Donavan kept his focus on the door, awaiting Donald's arrival. An entourage of about six men approached them and, as he tried to read the faces to see who was friend or foe, Percy called out. "Look! Donald beat the two a we here already."

The group was chatting as they made their way to a table. They sat at one with a panoramic view of the entire place which was something that Donavan noted was a smart move. Percy tapped him on the chest and they made their way over.

Donavan was focused on one man in particular. He was stocky, about six feet tall wearing a weighty necklace that Donavan would have bet money was the purest 24 karat Italian gold. He looked dapper but not too concerned about his appearance to fight, if provoked. He had a face that commanded respect and deep set eyes that Donavan knew missed nothing.

He was about to greet this man when Percy said, "Donald, this is my friend Donavan that I was telling you bout," to the short man sitting next to him. Though equally well dressed, this man was nothing to look at. He was short, dark-skinned with a collection of gigantic gold rings on his right hand. He looked vicious and the air about him was dangerous.

From the time Donavan first came back into Tiverly Gardens, he'd been learning many valuable lessons. That night was no different. He'd finally met the great Donald and the parable was never judge a book by its cover. Initially, he'd mistaken Donald for the help and not the man he'd come to see which was foolish, hasty and, if the circumstances had not been as favorable, possibly dangerous.

"So you is the youth who is selling on my territory?" He began.

Intimidated by the whole atmosphere and the smooth direct cadence of Donald's voice, as well as all the men who sat there prepared to do the don's bidding, Donavan answered.

"Yes, I guess so." He was looking around when he answered the question but when he turned the other man had not taken his eyes from his face.

"My youth," he knowingly said, "always answer a man direct and to the point when you is doing business, you understand?"

He nodded, not making the same mistake twice. He kept his eyes trained on the don now.

"Well, listen me now. This is how it a go work. Normally, anyone who sell on my territory, I destroy dem, make an example of dem. But, you see right a now a tings ago run a likkle different dis time. Percy tell me say...ah you have some ganja nobody in town have.

That's good. He tell me say he did what he did to see if onnou could make me more money, but first he had to try it out. Now, that it's makin' money," he said in a way that let Donavan know he was going to make Percy pay for stepping on his toes. "He tell me of it. So, see what we go do. Half of the money you make on my turf, you give to me, seen? And if anybody give you a problem, me send Percy or some of my boys to handle it."

The two of them shook on it. Donavan felt as though he were being taken advantage of but didn't yet see how he could get any better deal. He decided to focus on the positive that had come of it. First of all, he had sold on Donald's territory and lived. And secondly, he was officially in a partnership with Donald. That made him feel a little better until he thought of the fact that Donald was a boss type individual and that he had agreed to work for him in Tiverly. He was now working for Donald.

The crew ordered a few more rounds and Donavan drank a few more beers and got on his way, thanking Donald sincerely before departing.

That night Donavan lay in his bed thinking. He felt such a mix of emotions. On the one hand, he was floating on cloud nine. He felt invincible since he officially received the go ahead from Donald. On the other hand, his young mind was in overdrive, devising a way for him to expand even more without having to pay anyone. He couldn't stand the feeling of being taken advantage of anymore than he could stand the thought of paying someone his hard earned money.

The next morning, bathed and refreshed, he headed for Pudgy's. The fat boy was happy to see him but a little too jovial for Donavan's taste. He had more important things on his mind than football and chasing after girls, which is what Pudgy had scheduled on his agenda for the day. Donavan played with him until it was out of Pudgy's system. Then asked him if he thought he could move ganja in his area. Almost at once, greed, which had more to do with Pudgy's character than anything else, set in and the aptly named boy swiftly replied. "Yeah mon, I need to make some money."

Donavan employed the same tactic as he did with Percy. He gave Pudgy the sixty forty split and a pound of herb. Pudgy ran through it sooner than either of them expected. Then came back for more. He supplied him with another bundle and soon things were going so well between him, Percy and Pudgy selling that he almost depleted his supply on the outskirts of town.

Business went on at a fever pitch for the next seven months. Pudgy soon had a network of people and asked Donavan if he could start giving out packages to his cousin Bigga. Bigga lived in the Arima section of Kingston and it made sense to start spreading out their enterprise. He'd met the fat black boy the year before and he liked him enough so he agreed and added packs for Bigga in his calculations and distribution. A year had gone past since the meeting with Donald and everything was going smoother than he could have even asked for. Even though he was forced to split his earnings three ways from the Zanzibar, he more than made up for it with the profits from his dealings with Pudgy and Bigga.

CHAPTER ELEVEN

Donavan turned seventeen years old. His birthday, the first of November, passed with extra fan fare since he was making money. He had the best of everything befitting a Scorpio. He had beautiful women of every shade and variety, power, status in the street and all the money he could spend. But, he still wanted more.

Still a little groggy and hung-over from his happy birthday, the next morning. He paid a little kid knocking at his door a pound for a note summoning him to a meeting with Donald.

Donavan arrived puzzled as to why he had been beckoned but Donald had never asked him for anything, let alone anything frivolous so he sat down and gave the man an impartial hearing.

"There is an older man, name Popa Jed who been selling in my territory and saying that he work for me. I want you to find him and kill him. In fact take Thomas here with you he knows what he looks like."

Donavan couldn't believe what he'd just heard. The hairs on the back of his neck were standing. He felt a cold chill through his body when he heard Donald say he wanted an enemy dead and had chosen him to take part in the killing. Donavan made his mind up right then and there. Not only was he going to play a role in the killing... he was going to do it himself. He figured that since this matter with Poppa Jed was in regard to the ganja trade then that must be the reason why Donald chose him for the task at hand.

He knew a chance to elevate himself in the ranks of the underworld when he saw it and that was his chance. Thomas drove to the area of Tivoli where they'd heard Popa Jed was selling ganja. Then waited to see if they could spot him. They waited for about three hours and had no luck. Finally, after a little over five hours of waiting, Thomas spotted Jed posted up on the corner about to start his work day. Thomas reached in the glove compartment and passed Percy a black semi automatic Ruger and was about to hand another gun to Donavan. However, Donavan informed Thomas that he had his own piece. Thomas instructed the duo to walk up to him and ask him for some ganja. Then, when he reached in his pocket or stash spot for the ganja, shoot him.

Percy had killed on behalf of Donald several times before. He'd become used to the way it felt after he'd killed someone, but he wasn't too sure about Donavan. In fact, as they made their way out the car slowly walking toward Poppa Jed, he asked Donavan if he wanted him to do the shooting. In reply, Donavan just sucked his teeth and shook his head in disbelief at the question Percy had just asked him. A minute later, they stood face to face with Jed. Percy was just about to ask him about the ganja when, all of a sudden, he heard what sounded like strikes of thunder.

He'd heard thunder alright, the thunder of Donavan's .38 revolver. Donavan didn't waste any time on a discussion. To him their mission was a simple one: find their target and kill him. After the shots rang out and Poppa Jed's body lay in the street, the two of them high tailed it back to the car. They sped off making haste and Donavan was sitting next to Thomas in the front seat. Thomas appeared to be a trifle bit excited and also seemed to be talking, but Donavan couldn't hear a thing. He could only hear the loud piercing high pitched ring from the gun blast in his ears. Percy was talking to him too from the back seat patting him on the back for a job well done. Both the men's words were muffled because of the ringing in his ears. However, his sight was perfectly in tact. All he could see was the orange and blue flame from his gun and fragments of his victim's skull and brain matter flying out of the man's head. As well as the cold and lifeless look on the man's face before his body even hit the ground. He still could feel the rush he got from the gun jerking in his hand until he was out of bullets. When all it would do is just click several times before he realized he was out of bullets. He sat there in the passenger seat amazed by all that had transpired which seemed to be in slow motion but had actually only took seconds.

About ten minutes later, Thomas pulled over, parked the car they were in and told both Percy and Donavan to get out. Thomas went behind a house that was owned by Donald and pulled up in a completely different car. He told the two of them to hop in. By then, the ringing in Donavan's ears had stopped being as loud so he could hear a little better.

They made their way back to Donald's main house to report on what had just happened. Donald was pleased with the news. Percy was proud of Donavan but, at the same time, shocked because he not only shot Jed but just coldly walked up on him and started firing without saying so much as a peep. Now, there wasn't a shadow of doubt in Percy's mind that his one time protégé was a stone cold killer. Before he committed the deed, Percy wondered how Donavan would act when shots were fired. By all means, after he'd seen Donavan's work, all doubts were removed from his mind.

In the wake of Poppa Jed's demise and, on the strength of how Donavan handled that situation, he became closer to Donald. In fact, Donavan stepped up in the criminal ranks of Kingston rapidly after that event. Donald was so impressed at Donavan's business savvy and the way he could execute a man without blinking that he made him his personal bodyguard as well as his vanguard hit man. From that November first on out, people who got out of line or fell out of favor with Donald felt the sting of Donavan's young Scorpio he had under his wing.

In fact, over the next few years, Donavan and Donald became so close that Donavan was made second in command. It was odd but, through his ambition and sheer lust for blood, he quickly became the under boss to Donald's organization. At the age of twenty one, Donavan gave orders to men almost twice his age. If any one doubted his authority, often times the penalty was a gruesome death and he'd make sure his foes' bodies were left on display in public. Through his campaign of terror, Donavan had managed to put the West Kingston neighborhoods of Tivoli gardens, Hannah Town and Areema in a strangle hold.

By then, Donavan was making enough money to move his family out of Tivoli up town to the nicer and more tranquil Kingston Six. His ganja empire had also been blossoming and expanding. He put Pudgy and Bigga in charge of all the ganja that was being sold in Areema, being as though Bigga was from over there. Percy was his right hand man and was given control of Hannah town. Also, Donavan's younger brother Dwayne was made errand boy and put under Percy's wing along with a few other soldiers. Donavan believed in working your way up to the top. He didn't want to give Dwayne too good of a treatment just because he was his kid brother. Besides, he'd learned the ropes from Percy and figured he could teach his brother a thing or two.

He also placed Dwayne with Percy for a couple of other reasons as well. For one, it was a show of good faith to his old pal. So, he wouldn't be discontent with him being made second in command of all of Donald's affairs as well as to show him that he loved, honored and trusted him. Although, Donavan was still very young, he understood the premise of moral amongst the men he controlled. Although, Percy respected Donavan to the utmost, Donavan still didn't want Percy to get out of line and have to be made a severe example of. So, he placed his brother with him to make him feel that much more important. Plus, Donavan didn't want to expose Dwayne to all the killing he was doing on the behest of Donald. Donavan thought Dwayne was still a bit of a mama's boy and needed toughing up a bit first.

Later on that year, Donavan got married to a woman he was seeing named Stacy. She gave birth to their first son Dexter shortly after they were married that same year. At the age of twenty one, Donavan had a family and was doing more dirt than ever. Until one day, Donald called him to his main house to talk to him.

Donavan came in the house and found Donald and Thomas having a drink of Scotch with a very serious look on his face.

"You wanted to see me don?"

Donavan nervously inquired because, if Donald wanted something done, he was normally relaxed and nonchalant since he knew Donavan could handle it. The serious look on Donald's face worried Donavan.

"Relax my lad there's nothing wrong. I sent for you because it's now time for a promotion for you!" Donald said smoothly and direct to the point.

Even though Donald had just told him he was being promoted in rank, Donavan was still a bit paranoid. In his mind, he thought the only position higher than the one he'd had now was the position Donald held himself.

"Listen there has been a lot of killing recently. It's starting to become bad for business. The constable won't be able to turn his head for the money we pay him for too much longer seen?"

"So see what a gwaan. I know you starting your family now. You don't need to be in front as much anymore. Mi know me can call you if I need you still though. Its time for us to get into more legitimate operations now. To cover up some of this money, some of this other money we been making. There is a man name Conroy who owes me a favor. He work right under the foreman at the bauxite mine cross town. The man Conroy tell me say tis him that do the hiring of new workers over there. I need you to take this job. You gonna affi work a likkle bit while you there, but not like a real job. Just enough to look busy seen? The reason I need you there is to get some barrels I have coming from foreign. I don't trust Conroy the way I trust you. That's why I want you and your likkle brother make sure I get all the barrels I'm waiting on. You understand? Think you could handle it?"

With an easy self-assured smile, Donavan answered. "Yeah mon, you know say me can handle it."

That was that and the next day, Donavan and his younger brother Dwayne started work as laborers in the bauxite mine. Being that Donavan already had experience working in a mine from the labor he'd done as a juvenile in the labor camp, he took to the small jobs Conroy gave him like a fish to water. He no longer had to do the backbreaking toil but, having once been on the other end, he was sympathetic to the miners and very knowledgeable. He made sure Donald got his barrels always.

For the next nine years, things ran smooth with Donald's whole crew. They were still on Donald's payroll and also received a check from the mining company. At least twice a week, Donavan and Dwayne took at least a dozen barrels of illegal goods including liquors and arms from the mine without anyone noticing. They worked undercover of the night and Conroy faked the invoices to cover the tracks of what disappeared halfheartedly. But, no one checked anyway.

Their operation went smooth as clockwork until May of 1960. In May of 1960, Donald crashed his car into a tree on a trip to the rural parish of St. Catherine. This had been a family outing and his wife had been at his side, in the front passenger seat. She died on impact as well. Thomas was in the vehicle and was thrown through the roof but he lived a few days at the hospital before he went into shock and died from complications of the surgery the doctors had performed on him in an attempt to save his life.

The word of Donald's demise spread through Kingston like wildfire. Everyone, from those who hated and feared him to those who loved and respected could talk of nothing else. Donavan and the rest of the crew threw an elaborate celebration for their dead don, letting off clip after clip into the night sky after his burial, saluting their fallen leader. Their celebrations were short lived. Donald was a man who was much more feared than loved in West Kingston. He'd had a twenty year run with little to no real competition over the years. However, with him now out of the picture, some of the others people who had been waiting for the day Donald died to come, now stepped up. They thought it would be a free for all and, within hours of the news of his death, all types of scavengers were trying to claim different lots of Donald's turf. For about a week, the poachers were met with no resistance.

In their foolish minds, this was confirmation that the head man was gone, his organization had broken up and everyone could simply take their share of his empire. They were soon to learn they were mortally wrong. Donavan called a meeting and it was agreed that, as he'd been second in command, he would lead the family. He had most of Donald's connects and he knew the turf. For a brief moment, some of the soldiers under Percy's control thought to challenge Donavan for control. However, when they thought back to how easily Donavan could kill, and what his work looked like after he desecrated the remains of his foes, they quickly reconsidered and decided to stay silent.

By the time Donavan was twenty nine, he became very much the strategist. He played things cool for a week and a half after Donald's death for two reasons: one was the traditional Jamaican custom of mourning for nine nights after the funeral and the second was that he wanted to see what rats would crawl out from their holes and take the baited trap he'd been setting after Donald's death.

Indeed, throughout the whole of West Kingston, there were all types of interlopers on Donavan's new turf. Even places such as the Zanzibar tavern and lounge. Where Donavan's career as a rude boy had begun years earlier, found itself infested. There were new faces everywhere and a general sense of disrespect pervaded the atmosphere as it was a free-for-all.

He made his move after the ninth night. Donavan and his cohorts unleashed their fury. The vast majority perished without too much of a fight. Others simply broke camp and moved off. Still, some fought back or at least tried. A band of ragamuffins had managed to wound or kill some of Pudgy and Bigga's men. They held their positions for almost a week until Donavan himself, along with Percy, Dwayne and a few of Bigga's soldiers from the area drove through with Tommy guns and unleashed a barrage of shots that scorched their enemy's flesh like hell fire. When the smoke cleared, nine men lay dead with pieces of their anatomy blown away or mangled. They didn't even look like they were once men but, instead, resembled meat in a slaughterhouse.

In the end, Donavan viewed them as halfway formidable adversaries. Eventhough, they died pulling out their guns while ducking for cover and running backwards.

Due to Donavan and his crew, the whole Kingston was put on a sundown curfew. No one could be out in the streets at night. In fact, Donavan and his crew killed so many people in such a short time that detectives from Scotland Yard were called in to investigate. When the smoke cleared, there was absolutely no question as to who was the new don of West Kingston. The aftermath of all the murderous carnage was a lasting peace in Donavan's territory.

In August of 1962, Jamaica became independent of England and established itself as its own sovereign country. By Jamaica forming a new government, Donavan prospered immensely! Now that detectives from Scotland Yard wouldn't be so involved in the islands politics, laws would be harder to enforce for a new government. At least for a while anyway. So throughout the rest of the sixties, Donavan aligned himself with political causes. Eventually, in the latter part of the sixties two grassroots political parties, the People's National Party (PNP) and the Jamaica Labor Right Party (JLP) were formed.

Donavan's foresight allowed him to see the importance of having friends in high places and political figures in his back pocket. Since Donavan and his family were well known and respected in their area of West Kingston, both political parties unofficially sent representatives to speak in regards to him helping influence the people to back and vote for them. Donavan ultimately didn't care about politics but was a wise businessman. He saw the importance of being bed fellows with both parties. So, he decided to balance his allegiance to both parties by burning the candle stick at both ends.

Donavan's main turf in West Kingston formed into a strong hold for the JLP. Uptown, where he lived, people were pretty much politically mixed. However in Region Three, where Pudgy lived, the people predominantly supported the PNP. What Donavan would do was send his men to do in all of the different territories where either the PNP or the JLP wanted their interest represented. Then they would beat and terrorize leaders and supporters of different groups he represented in that area. His plan worked so well because he instructed his men to wear bandanas or some other form of disguise to cover their faces so no one could identify them as having done the dirty deeds.

In return, the JLP who were friendly with the United States would supply him with an arsenal of machine guns, electronics and the latest designer clothes from The States. They would also turn a blind eye to his shenanigans, in their streets, if he or one of his men were caught committing a crime. Through the PNP, he was able to get Pudgy's cousin, Bigga, who had no experience with the law other than the times he'd been arrested, into a precinct as a constable. With Bigga as constable, Donavan now had a legal gun on his pay roll. Bigga being a constable also served the interest of his political handlers as well. In addition to granting Donavan request of making Bigga a constable, one of the highest ranking officials of the PNP awarded Donavan 30 acres of land his family owned in St. Ann's Parish. Donavan put the land to good use and grew a whole crop of his Blue Mountain ganja there. The people of the area knew who the crop belonged to; they had gotten wind of all of the bodies Donavan was responsible for and there was never even the slightest temptation to steal from his crop or to step foot on Donavan's property.

The PNP also had their arrangements with Donavan. Looking the other way when he did dirt on their turf was a given but they made sure Donavan wanted for nothing when he was in PNP territory.

Through it all, Donavan didn't trust Conroy. Once he was the don, he decided Conroy was no longer needed. Donavan made himself the Head Foreman at the bauxite mine. Conroy would have fought tooth and nail, if it wasn't for the mysterious sickness that was slowly killing him. By virtue of the fact that he had been foreman at the mill for so long, some men would have sided with him if there was a power struggle. They would hesitate to support any new contenders because they would always think in the back of their minds that Conroy was so well connected, he would win. But instead, Conroy simply withered. He had no energy, he lost weight until he looked like he was wasting away and couldn't hold down any food. When he finally passed, it was a mercy. The doctors said he had contracted some disease. The coroner quickly agreed and closed the case as a death by illness, knowing full well that Donavan had him poisoned instead.

With Donavan himself as foreman, he could fix the paper work on incoming and outgoing goods without a middle man. Also with his political allies, Bigga as the constable and having great power in the streets, Donavan was untouchable! Donavan also became filthy rich during this time frame. He had so much money that his family had to be moved from Kingston Six farther uptown to an area known as Beverly Hills.

CHAPTER TWELVE

In Lacaye, life was simple but complex. During the months that passed, Jean and Winsome lived quietly, working hard to do all the necessary work to make their lives bearable. For recreation, they explored the island while they awaited the birth of their baby. Things were simple because they had each other and they'd resolved to go back to Jamaica once they felt it was time to go back. Yet things were complex at the same time. For all of her happiness with Jean and her excitement about the pregnancy and feeling their baby growing inside of her, Winsome was terribly homesick. She had never been apart from her mother for so long and, in fact, had never left the island of Jamaica before. The farthest she'd ever been from the home she was born in was to the country to visit her relatives.

They also both had to deal with the terrible news Pierre delivered to Jean about his parents. Pierre had told Jean of an on going feud that his father and several other people who were missing from their area had with low level grunts that represented their local government. It was ill advised to go against these thugs known as the Ton Ton Macoutes, because they had carte blanch to do as they wanted in their political districts.

No one had seen Jean's parent or the other people who were missing, and they dared not ask of there whereabouts for fear of them suffering the same consequences. It was pretty much understood that they were probably dead. Although Jean tried to put on a strong front it was obvious that he was hurting inside, and his pain was also Winsome's pain.

Having only Jean to talk to with no T.V. or anything else she could use as a distraction was making her stir crazy. So she slept a lot.

Pierre's mother, Madam Marie was a midwife who lived nearby. She had birthed Jean and most of the other young children in Lacaye and everyday she came by to check on Winsome and bring her little trinkets and news. One day, as she was leaving, she told Jean she would be returning that night, something which confused him at the time.

Winsome had been having pains all along; contractions and sometimes soreness from the baby's robust kicking but, that night, she was particularly distressed. She walked around the small house incessantly, holding her back and moaning and groaning. When night fell, she couldn't go to bed, her back was too stiff and she was having what felt like small explosions in the base of her back.

Jean tried to joke with her, tried to tease her, even tried to command her, but there was nothing he could do to make her stand still or lay down. Her belly was still so small that he didn't think it was her time and he began to wonder what she was going to be like when she really did go into labor with minor apprehension. He was nervous enough without having her turn into a banshee.

"Winsome. Look at me, you have to stay calm," he said softly, like she was a child.

Aggrivated and sweaty, she held the wall with one hand and pointed at him with the other. She was about to tell him off, but a gush of water hit the floor from between her legs.

Jean leapt from the bed, truly panicked. Winsome started shrieking, yelling to him that something was wrong. The water had blood in it! He was at her side in a flash, trying to keep his wits about him and decide what he should do next.

"Madam Marie!" he said when he realized. "Winnie stay calm, I have to go get Madam Marie!"

She hated to be by herself in the dark house on any night but it terrified her on this night especially. "No, Jean, let me go with you." She pleaded weakly. She knew she couldn't move. Everything in her body was telling her to find a soft spot and lay down but she couldn't bear the thought of being in that house alone. "Jean don't leave me! No, let me go with you…Don't leave me, Jean!" she wailed.

He took one look at her and, though it pained him, he knew he couldn't wait for her. He had to go. He tried to give her the lamp but she wouldn't take it. Her arms were clamped around her belly, the pain evident on her face. He laid the lamp at her feet and ran though the salon, out into the night to Pierre's house.

"Madam Marie!" He called when he reached her yard. "Madam Marie!"

He was frantic, about to race to the back door and beat on it when the woman appeared calmly, fully dressed and carrying a big bundle of white fabric.

"Jean, cherie, I'm not surprised to see you," she said in Creole laughing.

Jean didn't understand the joke. This was his first time seeing a child born and, for him, the event was frantic and urgent. He raced as he walked with her back to the house, often having to stop and give her time to catch up. The old lady was in no rush. Having delivered hundreds of babies, she knew they were never born fast and, when they were, her God in His heaven guided the mother better than any doctor trained in Europe, at the most prestigious medical schools, ever could have. She knew that the woman's body knew what to do, and anyone else present was merely for the mother's psychological benefit.

"Madam Marie," Jean pleaded to her in Creole, "She is in labor right now…there was water…with blood in it…the baby is coming right now!" He couldn't think of anything else to convey to her how urgent it was. She smiled at him but didn't answer and, frustrated, he fell in step along side her.

They reached the house in what was ten minutes but, to Jean, it felt like an hour.

Madam Marie gave the bundle to Jean and signing herself with the sign of the cross and murmuring a prayer for the mother and baby's safety, she entered the home. "Go boil water. I need three big pots of water." She took the bundles back and dismissed him with a look.

Jean didn't know what time he'd have to boil water and part of him wanted to argue but he knew Madam Marie was the most highly regarded midwife for miles and that she also had delivered him. He held his reservations in check and went to complete the chore.

Her moans lead Madam Marie to Winsome. The young girl was sobbing, racked with pain while the contractions were so hot and painful, she was breathing in pants.

The old woman locked an arm around her waist and supporting Winsome's whole weight, she took her to the bed. She handed one corner of the fabric to Winsome and without speaking motioned to her that she should spread it over the bed as though she were helping her to make it. Winsome understood and still hobbled with pain, she helped the old woman do that slowly. The smell of clean, crisp Clorox and lavender filled the air. Madame Marie had boiled the sheets that afternoon, knowing from the shape of Winsome's stomach that the baby had turned and its head was low in her pelvis. She boiled them in bleach then rinsed them in lavender water and hung them in a paved yard between other lines of clothes so they wouldn't be soiled by dust, knowing Winsome would need them that night or the next morning at the latest.

When they were finished, Madam Marie laid out the other fabric at the foot of the bed and walked back around to Winsome. She undressed the mother to be from the waist down, letting her keep nothing but a small slip to protect her chest from the night breeze. Winsome wasn't the least bit embarrassed. She could think of nothing but the pain and the way something in her center kept squeezing so tightly and something else kept making her feel like she was about to shit. She felt like all of her guts, and everything in her body, would come out of her explosively if she did have a bowel movement but was relieved beyond measure when Jean came into the room and she could tell him what she was feeling for him to translate to Madam Marie.

"Jean, I hurt...wooo...wooo...oh...oh...Jean, tell her I am hurting...damn it hurts..." She said instead of the precise explanation she would have given otherwise.

Jean murmured words of comfort, watching as the old woman eased Winsome onto the bed. He moved closer to help and she stopped him with one hand.

"No, you take off those clothes and those shoes. You can't touch the mother with the germs from the street on you, she's open," she said making a gesture that would have been obscene otherwise. "You can kill her with the germs from outside."

There was no one in the world as superstitious as a Haitian midwife. Many of them had never been to school or been formally educated. It was a wise art passed from older midwives to the girls they chose, based on whatever mystical criteria they established and, though it seemed as what they did was very primitive, these women had techniques and small ways that modern medicine would someday, a long time from then, come to know.

They knew how to sterilize an environment. How to cut the perineum if it needed to be so the mother healed nice and tight. How to get babies to turn, how to tell if labor was progressing and so many other secrets. Jean didn't understand and part of him wanted to argue, but he had no experience or knowledge to base his objections on. So, he did what he was told.

The next two hours were the most anxious of his life. Winsome cried, thrashed around on the bed, moaned and screamed and he was powerless to help her. He held her hand and tried to say comforting words but inside he felt useless.

Madam Marie sat in a rocking chair that he had bought from his mother's room, singing lullabies in Creole and telling Jean to go get this or that every so often. All midwives have assistants, usually a woman from the mother's family or someone they'd found on their own that they had come to trust over the years. Since Madam Marie had neither that night, she'd drafted Jean.

After he'd boiled the water, she had him pour it into a giant porcelain bowl, a cuvette. As he bought in each cuvette, she covered it with a sheet and sent him back for more water. When she had three huge cuvettes filled and the water of the first one was lukewarm, she had Jean carry it to the bed and she began to bathe Winsome as she sang.

She took extra care with her stomach, bringing the young mother to be much relief as she swabbed the warm rag around her belly in small circles. Winsome had been in labor for more than ten hours, counting the time before her water broke and, after that much non-stop pain, she felt like kissing the old woman for the momentary comfort she gave her.

She relaxed and felt as though she could sleep for five years, letting the motion Madam Marie and the warmth of the water soothe her. Then, she felt an explosive throbbing that made her sit straight up. She felt a pain that she didn't know was humanly possible without dying and she feared that her body would explode or split in half from the excruciating agony.

Madam Marie gave her a knowing look and shushing her softly eased her back to the bed. She went to the door and called Jean Paul at the top of her lungs.

He was there in an instant.

"He's here!" Madam Marie said excitedly in rapid Creole, pointing to the space between Winsome's legs. "My big, big man is here!" She held his hand and did a dance, ecstatic. Her happiness was contagious and Jean made his way to Winsome dancing a little himself, psyched up for what was about to happen.

Winsome was no longer groaning. She sat up now, grunting and panting. Jean held her hand, resisting the urge to cry out from how hard she squeezed his flesh and the pain from her nails digging into him.

The old lady held her knees, at last speaking the one word of English she knew: "Push!"

Winsome looked at her, surprised, momentarily distracted and the old lady winked, pushing the legs further apart. "Push!" she commanded again.

With a loud grunt, Winsome pushed with every fiber of strength in her body. She felt herself tearing and another superhuman pain that made her want to stand and run, but she fought it. She knew it was her baby's head.

"I see him! I see his head. He's coming! Ha, He's here!" The old lady said to Jean. He translated this excitedly to Winsome but the language barrier had evaporated and she seemed to instinctively know what the old woman was saying. She bore down again, straining with all of her might and she felt something huge, wet and stiff between her thighs.

"Wow, wow, wow. He is beautiful! That's one big baby, one big boy! Wow, look at that man! That's a big, big man," Madam Marie said animatedly, even though Jean could see that only the top of his head had crowned. "Good job, Mommy, That's a good job! Wow, what a big baby! A big, big man, Let me see that handsome man." Then, in English, she exclaimed, "Push!"

Winsome obeyed and, with a big glopppp, the baby slid out into Madam Marie's hands. The old lady began singing God's praise, thanking him and praising the beauty of the baby. She did this solemnly as she signaled to Jean to come see the child. Winsome fell back against the bed, drained, still panting. "Papa," Madam Marie said to Jean, "come see the most beautiful wonderful strong baby I have ever seen. My goodness, you made that baby?"

Jean took him with a heart full of joy. He was still bloody, nose filled with mucus and white cream lined his neck and all the folds of his skin. In Jean's eyes, everything the aged midwife said to him was true. He'd known earlier that she said these things at every birth. However, in that instant holding his son, he believed it all to be the absolute truth.

"Here." The old lady said, giving him a length of thread. "Cut the cord." She didn't just mean this literally. Figuratively, the child wouldn't be his own separate entity until he'd been unjoined from his mother, according to Haitian superstition. "Don't cut it too short. He will not be blessed. He will be stingy and mean if it's too short but don't make it too long. He will grow up to be a crybaby and a momma's boy if it's too long."

Jean wanted to protest that he did not know what he was doing but she wouldn't hear of it. Using his instinct, he tied the thread tightly around the cord several times then cinched it until his son was severed from Winsome's body.

Winsome watched this with hooded eyes. She was tired but the pain began again and she knew something else was happening.

Madam Marie would have normally delivered the placenta as the father or sometimes mother- in-law held the newborn but she knew it wasn't over yet. She rubbed Winsome's stomach again. "Papa, we are not finished yet. Tell Manman we need one more push…"

The rapid fire contractions began again and Winsome felt herself growing dizzy from all the things that were happening to her body. Through the pain and tenderness, she found her strength and grunting like a wounded animal she gave it her all. With her man and her oldest son at her side, she pushed the second twin out into the world twenty seven minutes after the first.

CHAPTER THIRTEEN

Back in Jamaica, the night filled with screams of pain and suffering as Donavan Vassel was on a rampage. Since the day he'd taken the boys to Back-O-Wall, the killings hadn't ceased. He'd known the word of Dexter's being hospitalized would spread like wild fire and that some might take it as though the Vassels had taken a loss and were the sort to be trifled with. He could never allow that! He'd gone instead into his own form of damage control mode and initiated a bloody orgy of suffering. Instead of waiting to see who would try and test him, he called up all his most ruthless killers and muscle except for Bigga and Percy.

He instructed the men to collect all outstanding debts immediately. He increased his extortion rates and he regulated every rude boy in his territory with new dues. If any one gave any of the men he sent out to carry these orders any lip, his men were ordered to give them a lick to the eye with the butt of their guns. For anyone who wanted to take it further after that, the penalty was to be death! And, it was carried out immediately. He wanted them killed brutally, and publicly.

Businesses that were late with the protection money weren't given even one warning. A man came to collect, got an excuse and left. Shortly thereafter, bullets rained through the window of the store or they began to smell smoke, only to discover both of the business' doors had been doused in gasoline and lit on fire. Anyone who mentioned Dexter was killed on the spot. Even old women knew better than to so much as ask about him or his condition after that first day of terror.

Jean stood over Winsome as she nursed Peter. They had named the oldest twin, the one around whose wrist Madam Marie had tied some of Winsome's red string, Peter. He was a big boy, aggressive and he ate hungrily. Jean stood over them carrying Paul the younger of the two twins, his heart filled with love. Madam Marie had left to return home and the sun was rising, without them having slept a wink but no one was tired. The young baby in his arms slept soundly, having been lulled to bed by the mid wife's song: "Feh dodo ti bebe, feh dodo." The lullaby, which Jean had sung to him so many times as a baby in his father's arms, stirred so many memories in Jean and he realized that life had come full circle. He remembered his father's voice singing softly even though he was just a baby.

The babies were swaddled tightly in the white cotton and they looked like little packages. The midwife had shown Jean how to do this after she'd buried the afterbirth. Jean didn't understand all of the rituals and all of the intricate details in the customs associated with childbirth but he felt a respect for life that wouldn't allow him to ignore them. Grudgingly, he listened to all the things the old woman told him, as she didn't feel that postpartum care was a father's responsibility, and he did his best to keep them all organized in his mind. The old woman would return. She'd gone home to clean her home and see to the children in her care as well as to cook.

In Haiti, there was no sense that the birth of children was a private matter between a man and a woman or that you had to be a blood relative to care for someone who had just given birth. That was the duty of all of the women and Madam Marie assured Jean that, for the next few months, there would be no shortage of food being brought for him as his wife couldn't cook and that there would be a bevy of soups for her to help her regain her strength quickly and produce enough milk for two big boys. He was happy and content.

Winsome was tired, drained and weak. She gave him a small smile, bringing the boy closer to her. The question that Jean knew she was going to ask sooner or later came softly. "Now that the pickney have been born, how much longer till we go back a yard? I miss my Mama, you know?"

He knew that he had no idea what to do for her and that she needed someone around her who understood what was going on and who spoke her language. "I miss Moma, Jean. She'll be so proud to see the two a we have twins!" She smiled hard, showing Jean all of her teeth and asked excitedly. "So, how long till all we can go?"

Jean went over all the arrangements he would have to make in his mind. He gave her the best answer he had. "Soon come...soon come. Lets give it another month or so, to let the babies grow just a bit and for us to get used to taking care of them. Then, we can go." He was thinking that by the time they returned, about eight months would have passed and things will have cooled down.

Winsome wanted to go back home that very second. She missed her mother, her own bed and the place she'd known as home since birth. She reluctantly agreed with Jean. But, as she thought about being a mother, she reasoned that she had to think not only for herself, but also about what was best for her children. And, although they weren't married in a church, she considered Jean her husband and had to think in terms of being the best wife and mother she could be. She still wasn't happy though. She sucked her teeth and mumbled, "Ooh alright...you promise?"

Jean smiled at her. "I promise."

CHAPTER FOURTEEN

From that conversation, Jean started making the preparations in his mind for their departure from Haiti. He too was being more considerate now that he had a family. As much as he would have liked to stay in Haiti and look for his parents, he was forced to face reality. It had been a little over seven months since he had been back in Lacaye and they hadn't heard a word about his parents. There wasn't any trouble from the Ton Ton Macoutes either. But, he didn't want to press his luck any further so it was definitely time to move on.

Pierre came to check on Jean and his new brood. Jean explained that he needed safe passage back to Jamaica for him and his family. Pierre explained that he had a connection to a smuggling ring that could definitely get them back to Jamaica for twenty-five hundred gourdes, which was worth a little more than $500 American dollars. The deal was almost done when Jean made one more special request. He wanted Pierre to get him an automatic .45 caliber with three clips of ammunition. Jean wasn't absolutely sure what was waiting for him back in Jamaica but he would do his best to make damned sure he was ready.

Three weeks passed. The new parents got accustomed to their twins and the babies, identical except for the small string on Peter's wrist, bonded with them. Soon, they could tell the baby's apart without seeing their wrists and the boys learned to respond to Winsome's voice. They also had an immediate urge to be near each other. If Winsome held one at the end of a room and Jean held another in the opposite end of the room, they would fuss. If they separated them further than that, they'd both cry at the top of their lungs until they were blue in the face. Jean found that remarkable. He had heard all types of stories of twins feeling each other's pain and having some form of telepathic connection but never thought it was actually true. Seeing his sons react to each other changed his mind. Winsome never doubted that connection for a minute. It only seemed natural to her that two peas from a pod would want to be close to one another.

Madam Marie and the other women told stories about twins every night when they gathered at Jean's house. Winsome still couldn't understand word for word what they said but she could follow from the expressions and the audience's reactions. They all thought, she came to understand, that twins were magical and destined for a life of adventures.

When the day came to leave, there were tears and good wishes from so many people that Winsome couldn't contain her own emotions. Life was so interconnected in the village of Lacaye that everyone knew one another's comings and goings. Jean and Winsome being the new parents with the twins were like celebrities to them. When word got out that they were leaving to take the babies home to see Winsome's mother, everyone who'd known them, even in passing, came to wish them well and kiss the babies. She cried too and it was bittersweet leaving Haiti.

They rode with Messieur Alexander, a smuggler who would bring Haiti's world famous coffee to various ports all over the Caribbean. Sometimes, he traveled as far as Florida and Louisiana with his legitimate cargo and, if the money was right, he'd smuggle people out of Port Au Prince as well. The smuggler would take them to a small port five miles outside of the Northern resort town of Ocho Rios, Pierre explained. He had come with them all the way to the shore and, after seeing Winsome and the twins safely onboard the ship, he stood talking with Jean. Pierre had given the entire money to the ship's captain. He couldn't charge the father of his godson for that but the gun and bullets did cost Jean $150 American dollars.

They shook hands at the port and Jean embraced his best friend and thanked him for his help. He didn't want to get emotional but he knew that since his parents were probably dead, he didn't have very many reasons to ever return to these shores. He knew he might never see his friend again. They gripped each other in a tight, brief embrace and then Jean boarded the ship and Pierre saluted Winsome for the last time with a wave.

Messieur Alexander had arranged an area with several loosely filled bags of coffee for them to rest on. They also had chairs but as the mid- sized ship bobbed along on the surf, they realized it would feel infinitely better if they lay down and that's what they did.

Winsome was overjoyed about returning back to Jamaica. Jean had explained that they probably wouldn't be living in Kingston anymore but that didn't damper her joy at seeing her native land again. Jean had to figure out what was going on with the Vassels and that was too dangerous to involve Winsome in it. So, it was agreed that she would go directly to her mothers and stay there until he told her it was safe to move around.

Winsome didn't care as long as she could see the look on her mother's face when she showed her her twin grandsons for the first time. She also wanted to eat. She had a longing and a craving for breadfruit but not just any breadfruit. She wanted her mother's delicious breadfruit, the way she made it. Indeed to her, seeing her mother would be like Christmas, her birthday and Carnival all rolled into one. She was positively glowing inside.

The babies slept most of the way there. Winsome sang the lullaby she had heard Madam Marie sing so many times: "fay doh doh ti bebe, fay doh doh…" until they were in la-la land and she could rest against Jean's chiseled shoulder.

When the ship docked six and a half hours later, Captain Alexander went above deck to straighten out a few details, cautioning Jean-Paul and Winsome to wait for him below deck for a few minutes. Shortly, he returned with news that it was safe for them to come on deck and leave.

Jean got their belongings together and instructed Winnie to hold the babies as he carried their things over his shoulders. As a precaution, he wanted his hands free just in case he had to reach for his guns. He shook the captain's hand and thanked him for getting them to Jamaica safely,then they started making their way down the pier then out of the marina to the main road. In the distance, they could see what appeared to be Ocho Rios down the hill side from where they were walking. So, they started walking in the general direction of where the lights were coming from.

After walking for a short while they were able to flag down a cab. Jean instructed the driver to take them to the nearest hotel. About fifteen minutes later, they found themselves on the out squirts of Ocho Rios at a hotel named the Ambassador. The rooms there were about forty American dollars a night for a double occupancy.

They opted on taking a double so the twins could rest comfortably on one bed and they could take the other. Winsome was ecstatic to be back in her home land and to be in a hotel where she could take a hot running shower after being in Haiti for so long with less convenient amenities.

Once they got every thing situated in the room, Jean told Winsome she could hop in the shower first. Before she left from her mother's house taking a shower was no big deal. However, she wouldn't just be washing away dirt but she was also washing away the feeling being a refugee and the pain of suddenly being up rooted from her home, even though it was by choice.

Winsome moaned and rejoiced in pleasure as every single bead of hot water touched and massaged her soft skin. It may have been only a little under a year since she took a shower, but not having to go to the well and boil water to bathe was priceless. Winsome stayed in the shower moaning for at least a half an hour. When Winsome finally emerged from the bathroom door, a gust of steam came out. She came out with a towel wrapped around her head and torso smiling from ear to ear, looking born again like the Phoenix rising from its ashes.

"Winnnie what happened fi you, you moan and groan in there like a man was in there with you. You make me jealous out here...I was ready to break down the door. You all right?"

"Yeah baby...I'm fine it's just me nah have a shower like this in a long time" Winsome replied coyly. As Winsome looked in the mirror and got herself together, she seemed to be glowing inside and out.

It had been a very long time since Jean saw Winsome full of glee and back to being "Winsome." He figured that, since they never had an official honeymoon and they were in Ocho Rios, they may as well have a mini-vacation. Even after all the traveling and spending, Jean still had a little over $4,000.00 American dollar's left. He worked hard to earn his money and couldn't think of a better way of spending some of it than enjoying himself with his family.

A short while after Winsome got out of the shower, Jean hopped in. By the time he was ready to get in bed, Winsome was already half asleep but still managed to ask, "Are we going to see mama in the morning?"

"Soon come... get some rest and we'll talk about it in the morning." Jean replied as he put his hand on her forehead and closed her eye lids for her.

Morning came much faster than either one of them could have expected. The sound of the boys woke both their parents only four hours later at about six thirty. Winsome went over to the bed and picked up Peter and immediately started nursing him. Jean picked up Paul and held him by his left shoulder till it was his turn to get fed. Once the twins were fed, Winsome was hungry herself and wanted some breakfast too.

About an hour had passed since Winsome began nursing the boys. Jean went down stairs to look and see what the hotel offered in its culinary repertoire. While downstairs, he also went to the front desk to pay for another couple of nights. While he was in the perimeter of the hotel for any suspicious looking people, he thought may have been in the same league as the Vassels. While downstairs, Jean was told that they could have breakfast served to them in their dining hall.

Jean went back up stairs and told Winsome to get herself and the twins together because they were going to be served breakfast. Once they made their way downstairs and strolled through the lobby, Winsome spotted a house phone and asked could she call her mother. Jean instructed the manager at the front desk to charge the call to their room. Winsome called her mother's number only to find that it had been disconnected. She thought that in her haste to speak to her mother that she had dialed the wrong number. However, after redialing the number several times, she discovered that it was indeed disconnected. She found it a bit strange but thought that since she wasn't there to pay the bill like she always did, her mother probably let the bills accumulate until they disconnected her. No big deal. It would make her return to Kingston that much more of a surprise, Winsome figured.

One of the hotel's bellhops escorted them into the dining hall and seated them after Winsome finished on the phone. From across the large dining area, Jean saw someone that caused him do a double take and was walking in their general direction. Then, the man got right up on them so Jean got out of his seat and began embracing him in a bear hug. Winsome sat there holding the twins absolutely flabbergasted once she saw who he was hugging.

"China man whah gwaan...long time me nah see you! What you doing out here in Ochi?" Jean asked earnestly and a little bit confused.

"Well, after that night I saw you last, I packed some clothes and came out here. My father have family out here ya know. So, me link mi uncle and told him what happened and he got me a job at this hotel. I don't trust Bigga and me know it's not safe anywhere in Kingston... for any ah we. So, I'm just saving money while working here... Then, I'm gonna go live in foreign. I have some family in Miami on my Momma side."

"Poppyshaw! You really think it's that bad...even after all these months, it still nah cool down?" Jean asked with a serious facial expression as he folded his arms.

"True bredren...I'm afraid so. From the time you left I hear Dexter people dem...have been killing left and right. Damn mi never mean no harm... But, I shoulda never take you to play that game that day. Then, none of this woulda ever happened." China said shamefully full of remorse as he looked down at his feet.

"Don't worry mon you actin scary.....it can't be as bad as you say. Plus, without you I woulda never met me Winsome," he reaffirmed, striving to lighten the mood. "We stayin here at the hotel for a few days then we gonna surprise Winnie mama. She gonna be happy to see the babies. She gonna be happy to see our pickney dem. We nah go look for trouble... But, if trouble come looking for me and a war dem a want... then we ah war... trust me."

Switching the subject China asked if the twins were really theirs. Jean explained that the twins were actually theirs and that China was Paul's God Father and that he was actually named after him. Winsome passed him the baby and let him hold his God son for the first time. They stood there talking, getting reacquainted for almost a half hour before China asked if they were actually going to be eating the hotels food.

He wouldn't hear of it! He told them that the food was geared toward tourist and didn't taste the same as home cooking. He got their room number and told them that his aunt cooked a large breakfast so he could fetch some and bring it to their room.

They had to wait a little longer to eat but, in just a little over an hour, China had managed to bring them three large plates of salt fish, akee and dumplings. Jean gave Winsome her plate and put the rest of the food on the dresser where the black and white T.V. rested then asked to speak with China outside in the hall for a moment. "My youth, do me a real big favor... no matter how bad you think things are back in Kingston... please, don't mention any thing bad in front of Winsome. I don't want her to worry. We're on vacation here and are probably going to visit her family in the country before we reach back to Kingston to see her momma. If you wanna come, you're welcome. I have a little money to take care of the whole ah we so don't worry bout that... but I gotta ask you... do you really and truly think it's that bad that you nah want fi go back to Kingston with us just for a few days?"

China just stood there shaking his head in a motion from left to right to signal no or at least that he really couldn't be all that sure.

"Well, it has been almost a whole year... if we're very careful and only stay for a couple of days it probably won't be too much of a problem. Let me know when you wanna go and I'll tell my boss I'm sick and take a couple of days off seen."

"That's the spirit Bredren. That's the China Mon mi know and love," Jean stated as he extended his clenched right hand acknowledging China in solidarity.

By the time they came back in to the hotel room, Winsome had already finished eating her plate. Jean just laughed at how fast she scoffed down her food and sat down to dig into his food as well. No sooner than he sat down and put his fork in his mouth, a special news flash came on the T.V. and interrupted the show that was already in progress. It reported a mass amount of carnage and mayhem in the streets of Kingston due to the election.

The reporter stated that since the wave of violence had erupted that at least fifty people had been killed and wounded in clashes between supporters of the J.L.P and the P.N.P political parties. People who didn't have any essential business in Kingston were advised to stay out of town and that a sun down curfew was being imposed.

Jean got up from the bed that he and Winsome were sitting on and in a flash turned off the T.V. "Rubbish... Pure rubbish. That's why I'm glad I never had a telly before. They only try to control your mind with that damn thing!" Jean scolded.

"I don't know may be we need to go to check on mama as soon as possible, to see if she's all right."

"Well they are probably talking about the ghetto areas. You no need fi worry. I'm sure your mama is fine uptown. We are on vacation remember? We'll go check on her and surprise her in a couple of days. She fine right China?"

"Yeah mon! You know Mrs. Stuart is tuff as nails." China shot back noting Jean's attempt to calm Winsome down, with they talk they had in the hall fresh in his head. A short while after Jean had finished his meal, China gathered up his aunt's dishes then left. They agreed to meet back up at their room and play a game of Domino's for old time's sake.

A few hours went by before Jean and Winsome decided to go out and have a day on the town to see just what Ocho Rios had to offer. Their first stop was to a local shopping bazaar that was similar to Papine in Kingston. From seeing the environment on Ocho Rios's bazaar, Jean noted that it was very similar to Papine. He started toying with the idea with relocating there to the North coast. After buying the twins a couple of outfits and bibs his hustler instinct started to kick in and couldn't help but wonder how much money he'd make if he were selling his goods there that day. Jean couldn't help but see the irony that they lived on the island but were behaving as tourist in the bust tourist season. He also couldn't help but to think how much money he'd be making this time of the year if he was in Papine.

They finished up shopping and headed back to their hotel. Jean secretly commended himself on a job well done for getting Winsome's mind away from worrying about her mother by taking her on a mini shopping spree. She was in the hotel trying on her new outfits and commenting on how cute the boys' new bibs and clothing looked on them. Jean just smiled and nodded his head in agreement with everything she said.

Later, as agreed, China man came through at about six that evening with a wooden board and a small purple velvet pouch with Domino's in it. The duo played for hours on end and had the time of their lives. Jean said to Winsome.

"You know while we're here in Ochi we not so far from your cousins in the country. Why don't we go visit them tomorrow then we can all go visit your momma from there."

"That's a good idea... I was thinking the same thing earlier but didn't want to say anything because I wanted to see mama first. But yeah, I'd like that. That way they can see the twins."

That was that. The next evening they checked out and got a cab with Chinaman in tow. Then, they were on their way to the country. It took them only under an hour and they were there, knocking on the door of Patrick and Sonja. Sonja came to the door and received a pleasant surprise when she saw Winsome holding the two infants.

"Oh my gosh...look pon you!!! Is that your babies?" Sonja asked, excitedly before inviting every one in.

"Yes the both of them are for the two a we." Winsome explained with elation.

Sonja told every one to come in and they spent the rest of the night catching up on what happened in Haiti and how happy they were to see one another. Winsome felt like a million bucks being around her family and showing off her newborns.

The next day after breakfast Sonja sent the boys off to school. Jean asked Patrick if he thought Popeye and his van was available for a trip to Winsome's mother's house in Kingston.

"That's a good deal. I haven't seen aunt in a very long while. Why don't we go and ask him. The worst he could do is say no right?" Patrick stated in a jovial and up beat tone as he played with his newborn infant cousins. About an hour later, everyone finished freshening up and was ready to make the trip to Kingston. Sonja was the only one wasn't going. She had chores to do around the house and wanted to be home when the boys arrived home from school.

They made their way over to Popeye's and he was more than happy to agree to take everyone to Kingston. He'd remembered the generous tip Jean had given him before. He was also excited because he had an excuse to leave the countryside up in Saint Ann's Parish and visit the big city of Kingston. In addition to paying for the cross island trip, Jean also drove and offered to pay for the gas and everyone's food if they got hungry. Jean would have honestly paid for everyone to eat if they'd really been hungry. However, his plan was to make it to Winsome's mother's house quick enough so that Winsome's mother could prepare a piping hot home cooked meal for every one.

Jean drove at almost neck breaking speeds on the island's countryside roads and highways. Normally, the trip would take about three hours and change. Jean managed to reach their destination in just under three that day with Patrick giving directions and taking short cuts too. Even though they got there relatively fast, Winsome couldn't wait a moment more to reach Kingston Six. She was anxious to see her mother so she could hug her and introduce her to her grandsons, not to mention start a home cooked Jamaican meal for which she longed. All that stood between her and the moment she'd been waiting for was about forty feet and the front door.

Every one piled out of the van and began stretching their arms and legs after the long drive before entering the yard. Out of respect of the moment, Winsome and Jean were first to approach the door with Patrick only a few feet behind. They wanted to make sure Mrs. Stuart saw her youngest daughter grandsons and son in law first before every one else. Winsome left her keys the night she left in such a rush. She didn't want to knock to spoil the surprise so she tried twisting the door knob first. Low and behold it was actually open.

Holding Paul close to her chest with her left hand and steadily cracking the door with the other, Winsome was finally home! As she set foot in the house, the T.V. was on and she heard pots and pans clinking together from the back in the kitchen. With her right hand over her lips and making a shushing notion with her index finger, she moved inward.

The television was so loud that her mother probably couldn't hear them all come in the front room anyway. After she'd gotten every one situated in the living room, Jean, Patrick and Winsome entered the kitchen to surprise her mother. Holding the babies in their arms, the surprise was on Patrick and Winsome when they saw who was in there.

"Surprise Mama!" Winsome shouted as the trio entered the kitchen.

"Winsome is that you? Where you been?" Winsome's older sister Gwen inquired as she turned to face the entrance that Winsome, Jean and Patrick were huddled in. Taken a back and not at all expecting to find Gwen there, Winsome started to grin uncontrollably and, on impulse almost with a child like glee, began to skip towards her older sibling and hug around her shoulder while still holding Paul.

"A who pickney dem?" Gwen asked after she'd given Winsome a kiss on the cheek and started drying her hands of the dish water from the dishes she was washing.

"Oh, I'm sorry. This is my husband, Jean, and your two nephews Paul Conroy Baptiste and Peter Dwayne Baptiste," Winsome exclaimed, happily and glowing with joy. Since Gwen was there, she'd gotten an early present for Christmas, had every one she cared for on the planet in one house all together.

"So, where you been. I been calling here for months and nobody answer the phone. When I reach from Thursday gone, nobody was here and there was a terrible smell in the house. I went to the back and found mama!' Gwen said with her voice cracking and a tormented look on her face.

"How you mean you....found mama?" Winsome excitedly asked, clothing Paul tightly to her bosom.

"Winnie mi a come here from Thursday gone and find mama's body... What was left of her lying cross the bed! She was decomposed very badly. Somebody shot her in the head and bore out she brain. I thought it was robbers at first but mi never find nothing of value missing. Winnie mama dead and buried next to daddy now. Whah appen fi you where you been?" Gwen asked with tears flowing from her eyes like a fountain. She spoke through her tears and sobs as best as she could.

"I been calling for at least 8 months, but I didn't have the money and the time to come," she continued. "So, mi save some money for a plane ticket and take time from mi job. When I reach, I found Mama like that... the police said she been dead a long time and nobody miss her. When I couldn't find you, I thought maybe the same thing happen to you! What's going on? Why you nah been here and who killed Mommy?"

All Winsome could register was, "someone bore out she brain!" and "mama dead and bury!" She heard her sister say this over and over again until she felt the sobs start in her chest and the gravity of the statements turned her knees to gelatin.

Jean saw her fall back as she fainted with the baby still in her arms and his shock made him unprepared to catch her or break her fall. In fact, Patrick who had just learned that he had lost his aunt was the one who caught Winsome. She was out cold holding the baby in her arms. China heard the commotion from the living room and came to see what was going on.

"Move back, give us some room." Patrick snapped at China once he began dragging her to the living room.

Once in the living room, China and Popeye laid Winsome out on the couch. Even though she was still crying and sobbing, Gwen came out and took the baby from Winsome's arms as she lay there unconscious. As Patrick stood over Winsome fanning her with his hands to try and give her some air, Jean began to speak.

"Listen. It's not safe here for any one ah we. We must leave now. Go get your things right now. We must leave!" Jean said as he regained his presence of mind after hearing the horrible news and gruesome details of how Gwen had found Mrs. Stuart. Gwen stood there for a few minutes, not sure of what was going on and wanting some answers. Patrick had pretty much gathered what probably had happened to his aunt and took the baby from Gwen as he demanded that she go pack her belongings and head for the van.

Still sobbing and confused, Gwen seemed to become a little more rational and receptive to the demand of her to gather her things coming from her cousin. After all, he was family and she had just met Jean. Gwen complied with Patrick and went into the backroom she shared with Winsome as a child and got her suitcase which was pretty much packed for her to leave anyway. After all the memories she had of her mother in that house and the way she'd found her mother's dead remains sprawled out over her bed, there was no way she could have even thought of sleeping in her mother's room like she and Winsome would do so often as children.

In an instant, everyone crammed into Popeye's van on their way back into the country parish of Saint Ann's. Jean and Patrick's suspicions of how Mrs. Stuart died were indeed accurate. The night after Dexter was put into the hospital, Donavan sent some of his goons out on the rampage, looking for Jean and Winsome. They barged into Jean's residence but all they'd found was the key where he'd left it and one hundred dollars. They had ransacked China's place and found nothing.

By the way they found Jean's place empty except for the money and the keys, they figured he must have skipped town with Winsome and Chinaman. The only other logical place for them to check was Winsome's. They arrived and saw the lights on and someone moving through the house in the distance. Without hesitation, the trio of Percy, Chubbs and one of Chubbs' soldiers named Charles went knocking at the door of the home.

When Mrs. Stuart cracked the door open to ask who it was, Percy shoved the door all the way open, breaking the chain that latched the door to the frame, hitting Mrs. Stuart in the face. The impact of the door knocked her to the floor, unconscious.

Once in the house, they closed the door behind them. Percy ordered the men to drag the unconscious woman to the back room. They threw her across the bed and Percy began slapping her about the face to wake her up. When she came to several minutes later, Mrs. Stuart was mortified. She woke to three strange men, three large armed men standing over with one holding a large, chrome .357 long revolver. Inquiring of Jean and Winsome's whereabouts, all they kept saying was "Where are they? Where are they?" Mrs. Stuart responded that she didn't know, again and again. Every time she answered that way, Chubbs punched her in the face while Percy threatened her with the sinister cannon of a gun. Finally, after fifteen minutes of torturing her and not receiving the proper answer, Percy told her, "If you believe in heaven or hell, now is the time to make peace with your maker because I'm here for you and I'm your angel. But, not an angel from your God but an angel of death! Say your prayers there now mom!"

Desperate for help and too afraid to scream, laying on her back, Mrs. Stuart closed her eyes and began to mumble through a prayer the best she could under the circumstances. She heard the hammer of the gun cock back and the cylinder turn to put a live round into the chamber then, involuntarily, she peed on herself, as she squint her eyes even tighter. Boom... Boom... And, in one second, her life was over.

The two shots from Percy's gun were delivered from only about two feet away- directly into her face and forehead, blowing away half her head and leaving her blood and brains splattered against the wall and night stand behind the bed. The force of the gun shot threw her body back about two feet. The force of the blast almost knocked her corpse off the bed, leaving her sprawled out in the bed as though she had been crucified. The three men calmly gathered themselves, hopped in their car and went back to Beverly Hills to report to the don himself.

Even though he was furious that his intended targets had not been found, Donavan Vassel was still pleased to hear that one of their family members had been tortured and died a horrific death even if he did know her husband and had worked with him for years...

None of that mattered, though. All that was relevant to Donavan was exacting his revenge on those who would dare to harm him or his immediate family. Even if Mrs. Stuart did know where her daughter and her lover were and she had told Percy and his Motley Crew that evening, the outcome would have been the same. Donavan had begun his reign of terror over Kingston, especially since it was an election year. That gave him much more of an excuse and a license to kill.

As for Dexter, he lay confined to a hospital bed for a month. When he was finally released from the hospital, he wanted to walk out on his own instead of being wheeled out in a wheel chair. He wanted to give off an air of power and defiance and show he was capable of walking on his own. Pamela, who he was now engaged to helped him get dressed and out of the bed. As he tried to stand on his feet, he fell like an elephant being balanced on a house of cards due to him acquiring a bit of muscle atrophy in his legs. The force of his fall caused him to bump his head on the floor and have to be treated for a slight concussion before he was finally able to leave the hospital. He was mandated to stay in the hospital another day for observation.

Dexter didn't learn of Mrs. Stuart's execution until several days after he had come home. Whenever he would ask his father or one of his staff if they had gotten word of where Jean and Winsome were, all he'd be told was not to worry about that affair and to get plenty of rest because they'd be taken care of soon enough.

The reason being that Donavan thought it was high time and as good a time as any that Dexter made his bones, by murdering both Jean and Winsome. That way, any face that was lost would be redeemed and Donavan would know Dexter could handle himself and was ready to be elevated in the ranks of the family business. After all, that's the way he graduated through the ranks of the criminal world to build his empire. He also didn't want to tell Dexter anything once he could walk again because his rationale was: what's the sense of asking about it if you can't do anything about it?

After about five days of intensive therapy, Dexter was finally strong enough to walk on his own. He wasn't one hundred percent; however, he could walk pretty well as long as he had something to lean against. Then finally, Donavan called Dexter in the study and revealed that he had all his resources at work and was searching the whole island of Jamaica with a fine tooth comb for the renegade lovers who'd dared cause him harm.

With a twisted smile and a tone of great satisfaction in his voice, Donavan calmly told his son. "Well, you know we never find that whore Winsome and that Haitian yet. But, it no matter still… because we took care of her mother when we couldn't find her. It's only a matter of time before we find them and I let you take care of them personally, yourself."

"How you mean you took care of her mother? You don't mean... you...you...you killed that old lady do you?" Dexter was stuttering in disbelief at what he'd just heard his father say.

"No me nah mean we just kill her... she was tortured, then we blew her head off her shoulders," he said with pure malice in his voice and a chilling chuckle as he nonchalantly poured himself another glass of Scotch while sitting across the desk from his son.

"Oh what's the matter? You want to live as the don's son but don't want to see others pay the price when they need to pay? Well, let me tell you something. Fix your face and stop acting like a likkle pussy. Tis because of you a whole heap of people been dying, so we can continue living good and with our business. There's a price to pay for everything in this here world boy nothing is free! Because of you, some may try and test our organization... and me nah build this here ting up to be destroyed by your foolish actions. Yes, we killed her mother...tis because we had too. And, yes, I did it because I love you. No one touches my children and gets away with it... no one! I say my child even though you've become a young man. Well, a man is someone who handles his business. All your life someone else handles your business for you. Well, if you want me to see you as a man, you're gonna have to kill that Haitian and the whore yourself when we find them. If you are truly a man you should have enough heart to kill another man. Especially, the one who stole your girl, embarrassed you by damn near killing you and put you in the hospital for a month!"

Donavan yelled as he pounded both his fists against the table wildly for emphasis. "So don't sit here and act surprised when I tell you of the price that has to be paid when someone goes up against any one of we in this family. This nah game...tis the real ting."

Donavan stated as he stared intensely into Dexter's eye's sipping the Scotch. He was probing Dexter to see if he really, truly had the heart to complete the mission that had just been assigned to him.

With his father staring directly and intensely into his irises almost as if he was staring directly through him. The younger Vassel got up got himself a glass from the cabinet next to his father's desk and poured himself a tall glass of Scotch. Without a single solitary word, Dexter just shook his head up and down in agreement with his father's diatribe and random rants on the issue at hand. Signaling that he did indeed have the heart to kill, Jean, his new foe and yes the beautiful Winsome whom he'd once loved. In fact at that moment he'd love nothing more. Even though in his heart of hearts, he thought killing Winsome's mother was a little over the top. He only wanted to get who was directly responsible for his stay in the hospital. He knew he couldn't say such a thing to his father. Donavan would reach over the desk and smack the living day lights out of Dexter... or maybe even worse!

No one reported Ms. Stuart missing. Her remains lay in her home decaying badly for months until Gwen came back home to find her mother dead in her bed room with half of her head missing. At first she knew it was her mother but just couldn't believe it. However, after a few minutes, she came to grips with reality and faced the fact that it was her. The way she could tell it was her mother for sure was that, when she was murdered, Ms. Stuart had on her favorite night gown that Gwen had sent from New York years earlier for her birthday. Gwen's whole world came crashing down on her that December morning.

She reported the murder to the local police and one of the first people on the scene was Bigga. He was responsible for spear heading the investigation into Mrs. Stuart's murder. With Gwen crying and ranting hysterically, Bigga acted as if he were consoling her and that her was a shoulder to cry on, knowing full well that his real boss was responsible for her mother's death all the while. The police removed the body after doing a half ass job of dusting for finger prints and showing fake concern. Then, Bigga brought Gwen to the police station for questioning. Gwen told him that her sister Winsome lived and cared for there mother. She was also no where to be found and she assumed that the worst had also happened to her as well.

Bigga thoroughly probed Gwen to see if Gwen could actually know Winsome's whereabouts. However, with the horror of just finding her mother savagely murdered, her mind was totally blank as if she was shell-shocked. When asked if they had any other relatives, and where Winsome might be, Gwen was in such a deep shock not knowing who to trust she responded no. Her carefulness not to reveal they actually had family in the country parish of Saint Ann worked in her family's advantage because, if she had, everyone in that house very well was going to be next to be murdered. Gwen's saving grace was that she just arrived in from The States and couldn't possibly know what was going on.

Also with the murder of a beloved older member of the uptown community there'd be too much heat and too much to explain if Gwen suddenly came up missing also. Bigga planned to wait a brief while before him or some of Donavan's other goons actually killed her. She was valuable because she could possibly serve as bait or lead Donavan's men to where the others were.

After over two hours of being questioned and interviewed by detectives, Gwen was free to go. Bigga gave her a ride back to the house and also stopped by the market. He made sure to tell her to call him if she found out any new information about her sister or if she needed anything. She agreed and was faced with the daunting task of cleaning up her mother's bedroom.

She wet a towel and wrapped it over her face to help dull the horrific smell that lingered through the whole house and pulled all of the windows open. She used lemon juice and bleach to clean the bloodstained room. As she scrubbed the wall and floor, there met a strange chemistry of the dark maroon colored matter of her mother's blood, bleach, lemon juice and her own tears with each scrub of the stained bed room as she cleaned.

Once she finished cleaning, Gwen was forced to come up with a solution to pay for her mother's burial. She ended up rummaging through her mother's jewelry box and selling several family heirlooms so her mother could have a decent burial and be placed in a plot next to her father in a cemetery on the outskirts of town. She made the arrangements and her mother was laid to rest that Saturday. Winsome and company didn't arrive until the following Wednesday. Gwen was to have returned to New York that Thursday evening.

It was Wednesday and they were all crammed into the back of Popeye's van headed back to Patrick's. Winsome was in a catatonic state delving in and out of consciousness mumbling mama, mama. Gwen just held on to Paul as though she were holding on for dear life. She couldn't help but notice the ironic beauty of the moment. Indeed, she had lost her mother but, at the same duration of time, she had gained two wonderful nephews and apparently a brother-in-law.

Even though Winsome was catatonic in the van, in her mind she thought of all the time she'd spent with her mother and how much she really loved her. Winsome wasn't only dealing with the shock of the loss of her mother but also of the pain in her heart because of the majestic moment of introducing her sons to their grandmother would never happen.

The same amount of time it took everyone to reach Kingston was the same amount of time it took to get back to Patrick's in the country. Once they arrived, Winsome appeared to be in a little better condition, still sobbing and crying but not the way she had been in Kingston or in the van. Patrick explained to his wife what was going on and was raving mad. He said out loud to Jean, "The bwoy ya chat about…Dexter kill me aunt, so now I'm gonna kill him! You know where I can find him?"

Jean grabbed Patrick by the arm and pulled him outside so he could speak to him privately, in front of the house.

"Yea, mon me know where we could find him in Tower Hill every other Thursday. He drop off money to Bigga at a restaurant named Cathleen's at about ten every morning. I don't know if tomorrow is the right Thursday for him to be there but if it is, we can catch him there…"

"How you know he be there on Thursday's for sure?" Patrick asked suspiciously for clarity.

"Because the bwoy Bigga mi chat bout is the constable and we both pay him on every other Thursday to keep the heat off us. Bigga was shaking me down but me never really and truly know why he pay him off but he does and it's every other Thursday but like I say me don't know if it's the right Thursday."

"Oh it's gonna be the right Thursday for me to kill him but the wrong Thursday for him fi breath!" Patrick stated angrily with his fist balled up, breathing heavy as though he were about to fight Jean.

Patrick had made his mind up about Dexter already. He had to pay for all the trouble he was causing his family and the murder of his aunt. Even though Patrick lived in the country, he'd heard tales of how dangerous the Vassel clan was and some of their various exploits. That didn't make him waver from his decision to avenge the death of his innocent aunt. He asked Jean if he would assist him in the deed the next day or if he could just stay in the van, show him where he could find him and give an accurate description of Dexter. To that, Jean just chuckled and pulled his two automatic .45 from his waist band.

"You see all the pain that likkle pussy causin? Right ah now that's the only right thing to do. Matter of fact anybody that's with him to... dem a go dead." Jean said in raspy and maniacal tone. Somewhat impressed that Jean was on the same page with him, Patrick and Jean began plotting a plan to set in motion for the next day. Patrick asked Jean if he had any money to make another move after they'd done the deed.

He made sure to stress that Jean was going to need enough to flee Jamaica with his family again. Being as though he was from Westmoreland, no one in Kingston would really know his face but, since they had killed his aunt over a fist fight and jealousy, Patrick knew no place in the Caribbean would ever be safe for Jean and Winsome's new family.

Patrick told Jean that Thomas who had gotten them to Haiti also had connections to getting passports. He suggested that since Gwen was going back to New York the next evening, they should leave with her if they had enough cash to pull it off. Jean agreed and told him since it was still early that they needed to go check with Thomas about the passports as soon as possible. They went back inside after their conversation. Jean had given Patrick the money to pay Popeye for his services that day. Patrick pulled Popeye to the side and paid him then asked if they could use the van another day for a little more money. Normally, Popeye would have been stubborn and ornery but the extreme circumstances Popeye agreed immediately to let them use the van for however long they needed it. He didn't even want money. All he asked for was that they return it with a full tank. Looking around and seeing Gwen, Winsome and Sonja in the severe anguish, he did the best he could to help the family out. After all, he'd known the family for more than twenty years and was like family in a sense himself. Also, even though Patrick wasn't readily showing his grief, Popeye knew Patrick was devastated by his favorite aunt's death and was crying on the inside.

Jean tapped China's shoulder and motioned for him to come outside in front of the house. Once they got outside, Jean explained that he was going to be leaving the country the next day for New York. He explained that, if he wanted them to, Patrick and Jean would happily take him back to the outskirts of Ocho Rios where China's family lived once they ran an errand.

"You leaving? You just got back, where are you going now, back to Haiti?"

"Nah mon, I'm gonna get some visas for me and my family and we gon find us a place in New York," Jean responded.

"New York City! I have money you know... We should all leave together. What you say about that?" China asked in a frenzy.

"Yea mon, I think it could work you know. Almost my whole family with me if you come."

They went inside and started eating the meal that Sonja had been cooking. At the dinner table, Patrick told Gwen and Winsome, who couldn't eat a bite since the gruesome death of their mother, that it wasn't safe in Jamaica for them anymore. He told her they would all need to go to New York with Gwen if it were possible. Even though Gwen had a small one bedroom basement apartment in Queens, she didn't hesitate to agree for Winsome and the others to come to New York with her. The only alternative was for Winsome to wind up like their mother.

Since they had all agreed, the only task left was to get the passports from Thomas as well as to get Chinaman back to his uncles so he could get his cash and belongings together.

Immediately after they were done eating, Patrick, Jean, Popeye and Chinaman hopped in the van and were on their way to see if they could get the passports to leave the island once and for all!

First, they dropped Popeye off at his house. Then, the trio made their way to the dock where Thomas had his boat tied down. Fortunately for them, they were in luck. Only a few minutes earlier, Thomas had docked for the day and was letting his last group of tourists go for the evening.

"Hey mon! You back I see. Let me guess you need another ride to Haiti. No problem. As long as you have some money, we can go no problem." Thomas stated chuckling, yet still remembering how he liked the cash from Jean before.

"No mon, this time I'm afraid we affi come bother you bout the other side of business you do. You still do that, don't you?"

"Yeah mon, me still have contacts to visas. How many you need and for when?" Thomas asked smiling, knowing he was probably going to see another payday.

"We need five right away. How much is that going to run us?"

"Oh, so quick…that's gonna cost you a little extra." Thomas said with great delight hidden inside.

"Well, since its five of them, it should be a little cheaper right?" Patrick quizzed.

"Well see, right now since you need them for whatever reason so quick it doesn't matter if you need five or five hundred. I'm still gonna have to charge you about $1000 a piece for them."

Right as Patrick was about to open his mouth and give Thomas some disheartening words about the steep price, Jean butted in and told Thomas, "Come on bredren, we did real good business before, right? I paid you with American money then and I still have some now. How about I give you $200 American dollars for everything?" Jean had already calculated that the five American passports would have come to $250 in American money if he gave Thomas all that he was asking for.

Initially, Thomas was steadfast against the deal but then Jean flashed the ten twenties in his face and his insatiable lust for money kicked in and made him relent after only about three minutes of negotiations. It was just that simple and the deal was done. Jean once again paid Thomas half of it up front with the remainder of the balance due when he delivered.

That was that. Using the cash advance for fuel and incentive to rapidly furnish the necessary visas, Thomas told Patrick and Jean to meet him in the lobby of the Embassy Hotel in Ocho Rios in exactly three hours. Jean was the only one with a watch he confirmed that it was seven and the men all agreed to meet then at ten back in Ocho Rios.

"Make sure you bring everyone who is going to need the visa hear?" Thomas emphatically stated, as they all parted company. They used the three hours to run China to his uncle's house. The trip from Ocho Rios to China's family house farther in Saint Ann was only an hour so they only had half an hour or so for China to say his goodbyes, gather his belongings and get back on the road.

They sped through the Northern shore of the island like a bat out of hell. Reaching China's relatives house in a little under an hour, with Jean's statement that he would be left if he took more than half an hour at his uncle's house, China was in and out in twenty-five minutes. He still felt responsible on some level for the whole fight between Jean and Dexter. He made a promise to himself to be there for his friend and to protect him as best as he could even if protecting him and looking out for his best friend meant simply following directions, he'd be more than happy to oblige Jean.

Everything was going according to plan. They were now on their way to Patrick's to pick up Winsome and the twins for the meet in the Embassy Hotel. They made it to Patrick's in about an hour and ten minutes from China's family's house and Jean hopped out of the van and fetched his family. Winsome was still clearly shaken and distraught by the events that occurred earlier that day. Jean consoled her for a few minutes, whispering words of strength and encouragement in her ear and told her to get it together.

"Don't even worry yourself love, just twenty four hours from now everything will be alright. We will be in New York and we'll be safe. Just need you to be strong until we arrive in New York. We must leave now to go get passports to go to foreign, see me? I need you and the boys to come take pictures for the passports."

Gwen overheard Jean's loud whisper and volunteered to come along for moral support. "Jean, Winsome nah right. Just now we should all go together!" She said, holding one of the twins in her arms. Pressed for time, Jean agreed.

They made it to the hotel with a few minutes to spare. Patrick helped Winsome to the lobby while Jean and Gwen tended to the babies, waiting to see if they could spot Thomas.

Sure enough, a few minutes later, Thomas came strolling into the lobby of the hotel, holding a manila envelope under his left arm and what appeared to be a fruit Daiquiri in his right hand. "Hey what a gwaan? Mi nah see you either since I left you in Haiti," Thomas stated excitedly happy to see Winsome again with Jean. He wanted to chat up some small talk with the whole family but, by the look on everyone's face and the way Winsome's eyes were bloodshot, he decided to kill the conversation and get directly into the business dealings.

"Ok, come here to this table with me," he stated making a waving motion for everyone to follow him to a small table. Thomas pulled out the documents and told Jean, China and Winsome to sign on the dotted line.

They did and, within five minutes, he hustled them to a photo booth in the lobby of the hotel. One used by tourists to document their trip to have them take their pictures. The little black and white prints would make the phonies look official. Thomas had a friend at the Jamaican Consulate who had sold him the facsimile of the official Jamaican Visa along with the official seal of the government.

Thomas said he had to do something right after the photos were taken. Jean was leery of this because he knew how easy it would be for Thomas to take the documents with the pictures to the Vassels and set them up. After interrogating the man viciously for close to half an hour, Jean let him go with no choice other than to trust Thomas' word that he was only going to get the visas laminated.

Jean agreed and let him take the visas to the back. Thomas made his word his bond and came from the manager's office with the visas fully laminated. It wasn't totally farfetched to suspect that Thomas might have been setting them up but Jean came to his senses and realized that, if that was the case, they would have been dead as soon as they stepped out of the van. Jean Paul gave the finished product a thorough inspection comparing it to Gwen's then grinned in satisfaction and put the documents in his pockets. He asked Thomas to step out front with him. The two stepped outside and Jean paid him the balance.

Smiling like the cat who just ate the canary, Thomas said. "My youth, it is always a pleasure doing business with you. Let me know if you ever need anything else from me. Right away, seen?"

Jean gave him a hearty handshake and a faint smile and they parted ways. He got the family from the lobby and told them it was time to get back into the van. They did and, a few moments later, they were on their way back. It was time for Jean to activate another crucial part of his plan of escaping Jamaica alive.

Jean was in the backseat with Winsome, holding her hand and stroking her forehead while Gwen rode shotgun with Patrick and China sat in the middle row. Gwen and China held the twins as Patrick drove. Jean gave him the order to drive to the airport. Jean knew what he had to do and he was preparing for it every step of the way. He knew that his next move would make him a chump or a champ. Only that it wasn't a game to be played lightly, no sir. The chump in this deadly duel would end up on a slab in the morgue. And, by no means did he intend on being the loser. He planned on being victorious every step of the way. Therefore, he planned on getting the tickets for New York that night, not the next morning. He didn't want to be running around at the last minute trying to secure the tickets. That way if anything went wrong, he'd have a little more leverage and elbow room to move it around.

A short while later, they arrived at Ocho Rios International Airport. Everyone hopped out and started roaming through the airport looking for an airline they wanted to fly on. Gwen suggested that, since she was scheduled to leave on TWA, they all inquire at that terminal and see if they could fly from it as well. They got their tickets, and China paid for his. That was that, everything was settled in a matter for minutes. And, with their tickets secured, they made their way back to Patrick's house.

Upon their arrival, everyone was dead tired. All the women and children took refuge in Patrick's children's bedroom while China, Jean and Patrick solidified their plans for the next morning. China would stay with the women and children while Patrick and Jean went to Tower Hill to handle their business.

Patrick went into the closet next to the front door and pulled out a sawed off double barrel shotgun and two boxes of shells. China was to stay back and guard the fort with his life if anyone tried to bring harm to anymore of Patrick and Jean's family. Initially, when China saw the shot gun Patrick pulled from the closet, his eyes opened wider than Chinese tea cups. After a few moments though, he accepted his duty. Patrick further instructed China to leave the gun in the closet but to keep a watchful eye on the front door and out the window.

China nodded his head in agreement and assured Patrick he could be trusted to handle the detail. Then, Patrick went into his back bedroom where the women were and came back with a long leather pool stick case. However, judging by the weight of the object in the case, China and Jean knew it was no pool cue. A few seconds later, Patrick revealed exactly what it was a black twelve gauge pump. He always kept shotguns in the house for protection but he never thought he'd be using his guns to hunt down one of the island's most feared crime families.

However, at that moment, all that mattered was revenge. Get back for what they had done to his aunt and all the trouble they had managed for his cousin and her new family. Patrick wasn't mean spirited by nature but, if you triffeled with his family, you had a certified problem on your hands. The Vassels were about to collide head on with a major problem.

The three men stayed up another hour or two, before they were calm enough to go to rest and get some shut eye. They would arise at six the next morning, to be on the road for seven. If they drove straight, they would arrive in Kingston at about ten.

The next morning arrived almost as soon as the men fell asleep. Patrick was so anxious to get on the road he didn't bother changing the clothes he'd had on the night before and had slept in. He brushed his teeth and washed his face and told Jean he was ready to go.

Jean took his cue and did the same thing as Patrick. Within twenty minutes, they were at the van. This time Patrick took the wheel and Jean rode shot gun with a swift beep of the horn, they were on their way headed across the island in Popeye's van to Cathleen's in Kingston.

The two men shot the breeze as they shrieked across back roads and shortcuts to Kingston that Patrick knew. The two men shared stories of what had been happening with one another since they'd last seen each other before Jean and Winsome's hurried trip to Haiti. Also, they planned their strategy of attack. Finally, after zipping through the interior and country side of the island, they were in Kingston with only about ten minutes away from their destination. As they got closer, Jean's palms began to sweat and Patrick grew more and more anxious to make everyone pay for his aunt's brutal murder. They arrived on the block where Cathleen's was located. They didn't want to be easily detected so they parked in the alley in the back of Cathleen's. While they were turning the corner, Jean noticed what appeared to be several of Dexter's goons in front of the restaurant. He checked his watch and sure enough, it was ten o'clock on the dot.

"Patrick, the boy there now, you know!" Jean buzzed excitedly.

"Where? You seen him over there so?" Patrick asked as he parked.

"No, but me see his boys and me know he somewhere around."

The two men hopped out of the van and tied bandanas around their faces so only their eyes and the rest of their heads showed. Patrick took the twelve gauge pump out of the case and thoroughly checked it then cocked it, ready for action. The cocking motion of the shot gun was loud and menacing, so much so that it gave Patrick a tingle in his spine to think of what it would do to a mans' frame. Jean pulled both of his .45 caliber cannons from his waist band and checked his weapons to see if they were properly loaded and ready to go. Indeed, they were!

They crept up to the back screen door of the restaurant with their guns out and nonchalantly waltzed in the kitchen, which was in the back. Since Patrick had use of his left hand, he opened the door and led the way in. He held the twelve-gauge by its grip and let Jean in. The two cooks, in the back at the time, were quickly subdued by the pistol packing duo. Without a word being said, Patrick simply pointed his gun at the two and made a shh-ing motion with his finger to his lips. Then, he signaled them to step to the far side of the kitchen with a head motion and Jean waving both of his guns in that direction. While still keeping the guns trained on the cooks, both men crept closer and closer to the swinging door that led outside to the area where the waitresses and patrons were. When they reached the door and peered through the diamond shaped window, Jean gave a positive i.d. of Bigga and Dexter, who were both seated and waiting to be served.

"That's the bwoy right there so, chatting with Babylon!" Jean whispered. One of the chefs overheard him whispering about Dexter and the constable and grabbed a meat cleaver from where he was standing. Up to that point, he'd thought they were simply about to be robbed but now that he knew the don's son's life was at stake, he thought about the reward he would receive for saving him and he tried to make a motion at the two desperadoes. He decided to throw the cleaver at Jean, who was distracted looking through the window. The chef inched forward into position but inadvertently knocked over several plates that were also on the same counter as the meat cleaver.

When the plates fell over and hit the floor, the shit hit the fan. Even though both men were still peeping through the small window, their guns were still pointed at the cooks. Jean saw what had happened and on impulse he let off two rounds from both of his guns. The sound of the shots somewhat startled Patrick until he saw the meat cleaver in the cook's hand. Then, he let off a shot from the twelve-gauge and hit both cooks with pellets from the shot gun blast. Both chefs lay dead from both Jean's guns and Patrick's shotgun pumps to the torso. The force of which knocked them back about ten feet and left the walls of the kitchen splattered with their blood and small bits of their bodies.

Up until the plates hit the floor, they had the element of surprise on their side. Once that the roar of gunfire had erupted, there wasn't any use trying to pussy foot around anymore. Both Patrick and Jean burst through the swinging doors fully ready for action. Patrick quickly cocked the twelve-gauge, as he burst through the door with Jean right behind him. By then, everyone in the restaurant had heard the shots and was scrambling out of the way.

The scene was total chaos and mass confusion. Patrons and waitresses ducked for cover and scurried out of the door. Bigga, on the other hand, had started reaching for his service weapon from his holster while Dexter's men who were outside attempted to get in, knowing better than not to risk their lives in trying to defend him.

Patrick and Jean were ready to start firing but couldn't get a clear shot with all the people running and in their line of fire. Bigga wasn't as diplomatic. He began firing rounds from his semiautomatic nine-millimeter in their general direction. Several of his shots hit a waitress and a patron. The other men seated with him, Marlon and Roderick, the don's nephews were momentarily stunned. Bigga was aiming head level at the would-be assassins, firing repeatedly and only missing by millimeters.

Jean and Patrick both heard the bullets out of Bigga's gun whizzing by their ears and ducked sideways out of his line of fire. Then suddenly, they saw Bigga who was now standing up making a motion like he was still shooting but was not actually firing anymore.

Click, click, click, click, click was all they heard. He was out of ammo. Being in a rush to get the assailants and shooting innocent bystanders was going to cost him dearly! He'd run out of bullets. As he pressed the small square knob that ejected the magazine from his carbine, Jean took square aim at the six foot seven frame of the constable. A target that big was easy to hit even without a gun.

In horror, Bigga was now starting down the barrel of Patrick's pistol grip twelve gauge shot gun. He watched in fright as he saw an orange and red flame erupt from Patrick's instrument of doom. He felt the wind from the pellets coming from his direction before he was knocked three feet back off his feet and on to the table where he and the other men were just sitting a few minutes before. Patrick's shot hit him directly in his large belly, blood was every where. Bigga had shot many men on different occasions but could never imagine the pain of being shot him self. Although, he was severely hurt Bigga still wasn't dead. He began reaching for his utility belt in a feeble attempt to retrieve an extra cartridge of ammo. However, it was too late for him to attempt to retaliate... Patrick was still on him.

BOOM

There was another explosion from Patrick's shot gun. That time the blast of the pellets caught Bigga, who was lying on his back and holding his crotch. It also hit him in his right foot tearing it half way off. Bigga felt his own warm blood splatter and hit him in his face. In fact, there was so much blood that it managed to get into his eyes. He laid there on the table convulsing in excruciating pain where he died with his mouth and eyes wide open blinded by his own blood.

While this was taking place Dexter, Roderick, and Marlon began ducking, using the table and Bigga's large frame for cover. In all the commotion and jostling during the few seconds of the gun fight both Jean and Patrick's bandanas came off of their faces. All at once, when Dexter realized who it was with two guns pointed directly at him and his cousins, he grabbed his pistol from his waist band. However, a mixture of excitement and nervousness proved detrimental to the young Vassel. As Dexter tried to stand up from the booth there were several loud pops from his general direction. Jean and Patrick jumped over the counter which was directly behind them and ducked for cover.

They did that not a moment too soon. Right as they hit the floor, Percy and Chubbs, who were the two men Jean spotted posted outside, burst through the door with their guns blazing! Percy had his huge chrome .357 Magnum and Chubbs was with a black Saturday night special. The two were blood thirsty and were firing rapidly and indiscriminately.

Once Jean and Patrick heard a brief pause in the gun fire that was coming in their direction, they both popped up from behind the counter and started shooting toward the door where the men had just come in. Only Percy and Chubbs weren't standing by the door any more they'd managed to get to the table where Dexter and the others were. Briefly shaken up by the roar of Patrick's enormously loud shot gun, Chubbs loosened his grip on the gun he was holding almost dropping it. It was a fatal mistake which allowed Jean to capitalize on that brief moment. Jean rapidly sent four shots from both his forty fives through his chest and neck. Chubbs grabbed his neck, desperately gasping for air.

Chubbs fell to the floor profusely bleeding from his neck. He laid there on the floor next to the table where Dexter and the others were done in by Jean's handy work. Percy, who was also in the vicinity of the table where everybody gathered, stood there as if he wanted a show down with Jean. Standing there with his gun in his hand by his side, Jean noticed that Percy's gun was a revolver and was thinking there were a lot of shots fired when they came through the door so he could be out of bullets. It didn't matter. Before Jean could think anything else, he saw Percy turn his back to face Dexter. Suddenly, there was another explosive roar from Patrick's shotgun. The force of the blast almost tore a hole straight through Percy's back.

Percy was indeed out of bullets and knew he was a goner so, instead of turning tail and running, he decided to act somewhat nobly and protect the don's son. He knew Dexter had a gun on him and that Marlon and Rodrick were also carrying. He wanted to shield them and give them at least a fighting chance of making it out of there alive. What happened next was unpredicted by any one who was involved with the whole fracas. Putting both his hands in the air and throwing his gun on the floor, Dexter began limping from behind the table after he'd stopped cowering behind Constable Brown's corpse.

"I give up... Please... don't kill me and my cousins! Just let us go and we won't bother you any more. Please, just let us go... P L E A S E!" Dexter whimpered, as his pants were soiled by blood and urine. He was so frightened of dying he lost all control of his bladder. He was also bleeding uncontrollably from his groin area. He'd accidentally shot himself when he first tried to stand up from behind Bigga's body. Jean and Patrick began closing in on the last three remaining members of the Vassel clan. They only were about five feet away from the three men with their guns pointed at Roderick and Marlon.

"Come over here so!" Patrick forcefully commanded, speaking to Roderick and Marlon. Ever so slowly, they crept from behind the table and carefully stepped over all the bodies until they were side by side with Dexter.

"On your knees!" Patrick demanded the two flunkies hit the floor. They almost tripped over the body of one of the patrons Bigga shot. When Patrick made Roderick and Marlon get on their knees, he immediately knew he'd made the biggest mistake of his life by surrendering. Jean and the stranger had no intention of letting any of them leave alive. Patrick told Jean to back up then unleashed the full wrath of his shot gun on Marlon then Roderick, who was on the left and right side of Dexter respectively. He shot both of them in the face and nearly blew their heads completely off. In fact, Dexter was standing so close to both of the men that, when Patrick let his gun off, some of the pellets caught Dexter in both his knees. He was brought to his knees from the stray pellets and began screaming in unbelievable pain, cursing the day he was born.

Lying there on the floor, Dexter was learning the true definition of pain. Savoring the moment, Patrick and Jean stood over him with their guns pointed directly at his head. Knowing that this was his end, Dexter held his breath and tightened his muscles to brace for the impact of their blasts. He closed his eyes tightly and balled his face into a maze like grimace. Tears fell from the corners of his eyes into his ears as he lay on his back. Sniveling and pathetic, Jean and Patrick couldn't take his wining any longer therefore had no mercy on him. Patrick cocked his shotgun, ejecting the red and copper topped shell that was used to kill Dexter's cousin and placed a fresh round in the chamber. Then, the inevitable occurred.

Simultaneously, Jean squeezed the triggers of both of his guns, putting two slugs through Dexter's forehead, blowing skull fragments and grey brain matter all over the floor. Since Jean had shot him in the head, Patrick moved the barrel of the shotgun to the center of his chest, hoping to give him a shot to his heart. The force of the blast completely tore open Dexter's chest exposing his rib cage and sent blood splattering all over Patrick and Jean alike. After Patrick gave Dexter a shot to the chest, one thing was for sure. Dexter Vassel was DEAD!!!!

So much had happened in Cathleen's that it seemed as if hours had passed instead of six minutes since they had burst through that kitchen door. Without one word, Jean and Patrick turned around and began to jog through the kitchen and back to the van. Patrick sped out of the alley like a contestant in the Indy Five Hundred. Both of their clothes were so soaked with blood that, when they got about an hour outside of Kingston, they had to stop and make sure either of them weren't hit. They pulled over on the side of the road and after about five minutes of intense scrutiny determined that they were all right. However, it had been a close call though. As Patrick checked his pants legs for wounds, he shook them both and two spent slugs came rolling down his left pants leg. Two of Bigga's wild shots had come dangerously close to wounding him in his thigh. Patrick thought about all the shots that were sent their way and felt extremely fortunate that he was only grazed and not shot.

Neither man had actually killed anyone before. However, they came out the victor when put in a position where murder was to only option for their survival. Even if no one else knew who killed the son of one of Kingston's most vicious crime figures, they did their job that day and they did it very well. Oddly enough though, if Dexter wouldn't have said that Roderick and Marlon were his family members, Patrick may have let them live - at least long enough to tell their story of what happened that day. Albeit severely maimed, they would have still had their lives. He enjoyed making Dexter watch him turn both of their faces into what looked like raw minced meat from the force of his gun. The sheer horror on Dexter's face when he saw both of them die right in front of him was better than any climax Patrick had ever enjoyed.

They made it back to Patrick's house in a little less than two hours after they'd stopped and checked themselves on the side of the road. Patrick made sure to park the van in the back of the house so they could enter through the back door. This way no one would see all the blood that was on their clothes. They stepped in the house just a little before one that afternoon. Even though, they came through the kitchen door in the back so no outsiders would see their now dry blood stained clothes, Winsome spotted them and began screaming bloody murder.

She thought they'd been shot or stabbed by seeing all the blood that they were covered in. Jean comforted her, assuring her that every thing was fine. Jean spoke to her in a semi stern voice and instructed her to get herself together, because they had to start getting ready to go to the airport. She calmed down after a few minutes and regained her focus after she realized the blood on Patrick and Jean wasn't their own. Once she got the idea of them being shot out of her head, she pretty much gathered the jest of what must have actually occurred.

While Jean and Winsome were sitting down at the table in the kitchen, Patrick decided to turn on the radio so they could hear some tunes and calm Winsome's jittery nerves. Instead of soothing tunes, the air waves were filled with reports of a massacre of nine people in a Kingston diner. Amongst the dead listed were a constable as well as the son of bauxite mine foreman and political activist Donavan Vassel. Patrick tried to change the station several times however every station was broadcasting a similar report of the massacre in Kingston. Patrick quickly turned the transistor off. After hearing the reports and seeing all the blood over Jean and Patrick's clothing. There was now no doubt in Winsome's mind exactly where the blood had come from.

Once she'd pieced together what must have happened, a slight smirk came across her face while a comforting and soothing calm sprouted throughout every fiber of her being. Even though she couldn't bring her mother back she took solace in knowing those who were responsible had paid the ultimate price and were murdered. In fact, Dexter's murder wasn't vengeance. It was justice. Now, the universe would be more balanced again she thought to herself.

Initially when Winsome saw the blood on their clothes, she was traumatized and automatically thought of her mother's brutal death. However, after hearing the reports on the radio, her trauma rapidly transformed itself into vindication. Gwen and Sonja were in the living room up front with China standing guard by the door. The radio was loud enough for every one to hear the news. No one said too much about anything. Sonja just said it was time for Jean and Patrick to get out of their bloody clothes so they could make it to the airport on time. Both men took turns taking a brief shower in the bathroom. Washing away the blood they were both covered in from earlier in the morning in addition to the grit, grime and sorrow of the day before. Once they'd finished showering and got into a fresh change of clothing, they were covered by much more than mere garments. They were cloaked in the fabric of redemption. Patrick gathered all their bloody clothes put them in a steel barrel in his back yard and commenced to burning them. He wanted to destroy any evidence that could possibly link them to the scene of the crime.

After stirring the fire with a two by four for about twenty minutes, both the men's soiled clothing rapidly disintegrated into ash. Around two that afternoon the children had come home from school. Every one couldn't fit into the van so they decided that Sonja and the children would say goodbye from the house. After fifteen minutes of kissing every one on the cheek and exchanging hugs, it was time for them to make tracks.

They left for the airport and got there about a quarter to three. A mere fifteen minuates before boarding was to start taking place. With no time to spare, they hastily made their way to the T.W.A terminal and began checking their luggage at a fever pitch as not to miss their boarding call. Miraculously, they made it by the skin of their teeth and got to their seats by the time the final flight instructions were being given in preparation for take off. Then came the magic moment when the plane began to taxi down the tarmack onto the runway which it was designated to take off from. Just like that as if some one had snapped their finger, the white Boeing 747 started roaring down the runway. Jean who had never flown before held Winsome's right hand tightly with his left hand and they both cradled the twins with the opposite arms. The sensation of the take off felt like the back seat was going to come through their backs because of the sharp rapid incline. The plane tilted slightly to its left as it went in small circles to gain the proper altitude. When the rudder of the wing made a menacing mechanical sound, Chinaman, who also had never flown before, became visibly shaken.

Gwen, who was sitting in a window seat by the wing behind Jean and Winsome, was directly to the left of China. She began to stroke his hand soothing him assuring him that everything was going to be fine.

"Calm your self mon. There's nothing to worry about. I already flew back and forth to Jamaica a few times and there's nothing to be afraid of. They say flying is safer than driving you know."

Gwen started in a soothing almost mother like tone as she continued stroking his left hand and rubbing his arm. A few minutes later the plane stabilized and was at its desired altitude to reach cruising speed. About twenty minutes later, the captain announced that they were over Cuba and, if the passengers looked out their windows, they could see the island for themselves. Winsome was now comfortable and was straining her eyes to see the island from the plane's window. She could see cars and people and they looked to be the size of ants. The whole experience of flying was like nothing she'd experienced before, and was beyond compare to all other modes of transportation.

Shortly after Cuba was out of sight, everyone dozed off into a deep sleep, only to be awakened by turbulence. Then, the announcement came.

"May I have your attention please? This is your captain speaking. We are experiencing slight turbulence as we make our final descent and approach into New York's JKF International Airport. At this time, I'd like to ask anyone roaming the cabin to return to their seat and fasten your seatbelts please."

The excitement was at a fever pitch once the captain made the announcement. Winsome looked out of the window and couldn't believe her eyes. In the distance, still about two thousand feet below them, she could see the statue of liberty!

FIN

Stay tuned to www.Myspace.com/Maxwellpennonline for info on Larceny of the Heart Two: The American Dream coming soon.